THE
SLIP SLIDERS
CLUB

DAVID B ONKST

Cover photograph courtesy of pexels.com
free stock photos and royalty free images

brown-tunnel-19883
by Manuel Joseph

ONE

☁ ✈ 🌴

Somewhere Above Florida

Letitia Gordon experienced, if not the proverbial seconds of pure terror that punctuated the many hours of flight boredom, at least many minutes of heightened alertness. Her first officer, Lola Sandborne, seemed to suddenly be in extreme distress.

"Where am I, how did I get here, what the…" shouted Lola, staring at the instruments in front of her. Her heart pounded, there was a look of shock on her face, and her breaths came in great gasps.

The SolAir pilot had never experienced what appeared to be a sudden mental breakdown of a crew member. She immediately thought of similar circumstances where mentally unstable crew members had committed suicide while taking entire airplanes of souls along with them to their doom. It caused her concern.

"OK, calm down please. You are my first officer on flight 636 of SolAir. Do you remember now?" asked Letitia.

"First officer? How did I get here? I was doing research on possibly placing some stock options. What am I doing in this airplane in this seat? I don't understand," said Lola, her voice rising in pitch and volume.

"OK, just don't touch anything now please."

Seeing that reasoning with Lola was not exactly the way to go, Letitia quickly determined that it was time to take remedial action.

"Lola, perhaps you would like to go back into the cabin, maybe go to the restroom and splash some water in your face?"

"Uh, O.K.," muttered Lola, still obviously unnerved.

"Just be careful getting up, no unintended inputs, please."

"Huh?"

"Keep your feet off those pedals, don't bump the yoke, uh, the steering wheel; and stay clear of any levers, buttons, and switches."

Lola fumbled with her harness for a bit, finally unbuckling it. She got up unsteadily, weaving her way through the cramped cockpit. "How do I open this door?"

"Really?" Letitia also got up, leaving control of the aircraft to the autopilot. "Move." She opened the door and let Lola out.

As Lola exited and closed the cockpit door, Letitia called out to the flight attendant who was standing near the door in the galley area. "Jason, don't we have a SolAir pilot on board who's dead heading?"

"Yes, ma'am."

"Please ask him to come to the cockpit and take over as first officer. It's an emergency. And we also have an Air Marshall on board?"

"Yes."

"Please ask him to watch over Lola until I can make an emergency landing at Jacksonville. She's had some sort of episode, and seems in quite an agitated state."

"Uh, sure."

The Air Marshall came forward and took Lola back to the empty window seat near his. The off-duty pilot came forward, introduced himself as Jean Phillipe, and was pressed into service as first officer of flight six-three-six.

Letitia got back in the pilot's seat, pointed to the right seat and said, "thank you Jean. Handle the radio please. Inform Jax Center that we have had a medical emergency and need to land at JAX. We'll need transport to a facility with psychiatric care available standing by." Letitia spoke to the flight attendant. "Please close the cockpit door." They were secure and at full strength again in the cockpit.

"Jax Center, Sunny six-three-six."

Go ahead Sunny six-three-six."

"Declaring medical emergency, wish to land at JAX with medical transport to facility with psychiatric care available."

"Psychiatric?"

"Affirmative. Crew member with apparent episode. Please advise with vector."

"Steer zero-two-zero for Jax International. Will have medical transport standing by. Sunny six-three-six, descend and maintain flight level one-zero-zero."

"Sunny six-three-six, descend and maintain flight level one-zero-zero."

Letitia then got on the cabin intercom. "Ladies and Gentlemen, this is your captain. Uh, we've had a medical emergency on board. We're going to have to make a slight detour to Jacksonville to deal with it. I apologize for the inconvenience. Flight attendants, please prepare for landing approach."

To Jean she said, "I swear I can hear the gripes and groans through the cockpit door."

Jean chuckled.

Other traffic into and out of Jacksonville International, light to begin with, was held in place until their flight was vectored into a landing on runway eight. As Letitia turned the craft onto final, the pilots got busy with preparations for the unscheduled landing. Jean was calling out airspeed and altitude.

Gear down," called Letitia.

"Three down and green," Jean responded.

"Flaps twenty."

Jean set the flaps handle for twenty degrees. This basically made the wings wider and thicker, increasing lift, and of course drag as well.

They crossed over the threshold of runway eight, and as the large aircraft approached the tarmac, Letitia pulled back on the yoke in a maneuver called the flare, causing the plane to lose lift and essentially fall onto the runway, albeit gracefully enough it was hardly felt inside. If not for the flare they would have glided far down the runway due to a phenomenon known as ground effect.

Engines were brought into reverse thrust with a roar and toe brakes were applied, bringing the aircraft to a quick stop as passengers strained against their seatbelts.

"At least I gave them a soft landing," said Letitia. "Doubt that helps their schedules, though."

Letitia taxied the plane up to a waiting emergency vehicle, and rolling stairs were pushed up to the aircraft. The passengers were told to remain seated, all but Lola and the Air Marshall. As they went down the stairs, Lola looked back at the plane. Though not a frequent flyer, she recognized it as the ubiquitous Boeing 737, stuffed with cramped passengers 3 wide on each side, except for those who could and did shell out for business class seats, that got one half more room, split off from the missing middle seat. She was loaded into the transport, and the Air Marshall returned to the waiting jet after tossing Lola's bag into the back of the ambulance. The cabin door was sealed shut once again.

"Contact ground and let's get rolling again," said Captain Letitia Gordon. "We're good on fuel."

After getting instructions from ground control, checklists were gone through as if starting the flight anew.

They taxied to the active runway, and lined up pointed down it.

"...cleared for immediate takeoff," came the call from the tower.

"Six-three-six, cleared for immediate takeoff," Jean confirmed.

With a mighty roar, this time the passengers were pushed back into their seats, as the jet abruptly gained speed.

"V-one. Rotate," Jean called out.

The earth began to drop away, as the passengers now sunk into their seats, accompanied by the clunk of the landing gear retracting, and the whine of flaps returning to zero, as flight six-three-six resumed its airborne journey.

☁ ✈ 🌴

Lola had never been in the back of an ambulance before. The inside of the Jacksonville Fire Rescue van seemed like it was a rolling hospital room. Having checked her vitals and determined there was no immediate medical emergency, the paramedics proceeded to the hospital much like normal traffic.

"I just don't know what happened. It's like I was knocked out and came to in the cockpit of an airliner. This is crazy."

"I'm sure they'll get you all figured out at the hospital," said the paramedic. He wasn't sure if they would or not, but was trying to be positive. He had mostly dealt with car accident victims and the elderly falling and breaking bones to this point. He had little experience with the mentally ill.

Lola remained silent the remainder of the trip, staring at the ceiling, trying to fight off the panic that enveloped her. They pulled to a stop under the portico outside the emergency room, and wheeled her out. Inside she was processed and moved into a large elevator, which deposited her on the fourth floor, then she was put into room 412.

Nurses took over and helped her out of her SolAir uniform and into a hospital gown.

"Dr. Graves will be in shortly to see you," said a nurse, as she hooked up Lola to a saline solution intravenous drip. "Try to get some rest in the meantime."

Suddenly alone in her hospital bed, Lola struggled to fight off the onset of panic once again. After what seemed like an eternity to her, but in actuality was only twenty minutes, Dr. Leanna Graves strode into the room.

"Hello, Ms. Sandborne. I'm Doctor Graves. So, can you tell me just what has happened?"

Lola led the doctor through what had transpired, from sitting at her computer at home, to suddenly finding herself at the controls of the jet airline. It alleviated her discomfort somewhat to be doing something constructive, telling her story to someone who actually seemed concerned.

After she finished, Dr. Graves spoke, "Well Lola, I think you may be suffering from a condition known as dissociative amnesia. There may have been some shock in your life that precipitated it. Of course, you wouldn't recall it."

"But I remember my life before today. All of it. I work odd jobs and trade stocks now. What could explain that?"

"Perhaps you could be suffering from dissociative identity disorder in that case, although that's exceptionally rare. I can't say for sure at this point. We'll talk again tomorrow. In the meantime, we'll give you something to ease your anxiety. Try to get some rest."

With that, the doctor exited the room. A nurse came back in and Lola saw her shoot something into her intravenous feed. A feeling of calm fell over her for the first time in many hours.

Dr. Tomas Hernandez was a short, stocky middle-aged man, with brown eyes set above the beginnings of bags. A white lab coat mostly covered his casual clothing. He was prematurely balding, but insisted on combing over what dark hair he had left. He was making his usual rounds late in the day at Atlantic Beach Medical Center, when he overheard his colleagues excitedly talking about a patient who had just been admitted.

"She was a pilot who suddenly seemed completely disoriented. As if she had never been in the cockpit of an airplane, as if it were completely foreign to her," said a nurse.

"Excuse me," said Dr. Fernandez, could you tell me where this woman is?"

"Room 412. The name is Lola Sandborne. She's being kept overnight for observation. Dr. Graves thinks dissociative amnesia. Maybe even dissociative identity disorder."

Dr. Fernandez thanked the nurse and headed immediately to Lola's room.

As he entered, he noticed the look of concern on Lola's face as she looked up.

"Lola, my name is Dr. Fernandez. How are you feeling?"

"A little better now, they gave me the good stuff," said Lola, pointing toward the IV inserted in her wrist.

"I've heard about your situation."

"My situation? I don't get my situation. I was at my computer, about to execute a stock order, and suddenly… And when I went back to the cabin, none of the passengers were wearing a mask. Why weren't they wearing masks? Why aren't you masked? And then I was put in a window seat and basically treated like I was some wacko."

"Why should they have been wearing masks? Why should I?"

"Because of the pandemic, because of COVID-19."

"A pandemic? COVID-19?"

"Yeah. Has the mask order been lifted?"

Dr. Fernandez did not answer, suddenly seeming deep in thought.

"And I saw myself in a mirror. I'm not quite sure how to put this. I'm myself, but not quite myself. I'm dressed differently, and I've never let my hair grow out this far. How did that happen? Plus, I can't get into this mobile phone, it's not the one I own, and here's the weirdest thing of all: the date is almost five months into the past."

"I think I understand," said Dr. Fernandez after a few moments. "Actually, I have been in your exact situation."

"You have? Again, what situation exactly? Have I gone mad? I've gone insane haven't I. I'm hallucinating, right? I can't understand. How did I get in that airplane, at the controls, for God's sake. I don't have amnesia, I remember everything before that, I know who I am. I'm Lola Sandborne. I trade stocks on-line. I'm what you would call a day trader. At my home office in Fordesboro. I'm certainly not a pilot."

"No, I don't think you're insane. Your doctor has diagnosed you with a dissociative state, but I don't think so. I will explain in more detail later, but now I must complete my rounds. We'll talk again tomorrow. Please try to get some rest. The 'good stuff' should help with that."

"So, are you a psychiatrist?"

"No, I'm actually an oncologist. Again, I'll explain later. Oh, just one more thing. Can you tell me the date that this happened to you? And the time, as closely as you can reckon?"

"Uh, today."

"I mean, what was *today* for you?"

"Oh. March the 28th, it was a Thursday. Around four p.m. The markets had just closed."

"And the year?"

"The year? Well, 2020 of course." Lola gave Dr. Fernandez a puzzled look.

"Thanks." Dr. Fernandez pulled out a small notebook out of his pocket, scribbled some notes, then turned and left the room. Once well down the hallway he placed a call.

"I think we may have another prospective member. It's been a while, but I think we have another slip slider. And she appears to come from a near-dimension. Just as I did. Just as we all did that remained sane enough to communicate, and were able to try to adapt. Could you see what you can find out about the background of a Lola Sandborne, looks to be in her late thirties, about five-three, green eyes, reddish hair. First officer for SolAir airline. Soon, please. Thanks. Bye."

I think I'll keep the time differential part to myself, for now, thought the   Doctor.

TWO

⚭

Alternate Lola

Dr. Fernandez felt there was a sense of urgency in the voices coming from room 412 as he neared it the next morning. He quickened his pace and strode into the room to witness Lola breathing hard, a cannula in her nose, two people in scrubs hovering over her. He recognized Dr. Leanna Graves, her attending physician. He always had to remind himself not to make comments on such an obviously ironic name for a doctor, especially one as well respected as she.

"Dr. Graves, what happened?"

"Anaphylactic shock. Ms. Sandborne apparently asked for peanut butter for her toast, so it looks like a classic peanut allergy. It's very odd that she wouldn't list such a food allergy, and even more so that she would actually request peanut butter and spread it on her toast. It's doubtful she's never had peanuts before. There seems to be a lot of confusion on her part about her past, other than her name. After epinephrine she's doing better. Uh, Dr. Fernandez, what are you doing here? Aren't you an oncologist?"

"Yes, I took an interest in this particular case as it presented many similarities to a previous one I am familiar with."

"Well, maybe I should consult with you then," said Dr. Graves.

Maybe, especially since I have first person experience with that case, thought Dr. Tomas Fernandez. "Sure, just set up some time for us to get together," said Dr. Fernandez, secretly hoping to avoid such a meeting. "Well then, I'll see you later," he said, motioning for nurse Dylan Feldon to follow him out into the hallway. "Please let me know when the patient has recovered enough for me to talk to her," said Dr. Fernandez.

"Will do," said Nurse Feldon.

"Thank you."

⚭

Heading back to room 412 later that day after being contacted by Nurse Feldon, Dr. Fernandez considered how much to try to reveal to Lola right away. He came to the conclusion that no matter how bizarre it may seem to her, what he was about to attempt to explain would be no more disturbing and disorienting than what she was already going through.

"Good afternoon, Lola," he said as he sat down in the visitor's chair. Lola was sitting up, her legs dangling over the side of the hospital bed.

"I've had better. Absolutely nothing has made any sense to me lately. I never had any allergies."

"I imagine that's completely true, in your world."

"In my world? You saying I'm an alien?" asked Lola, her forehead wrinkled in total confusion.

"In a way, but not in the way that word normally implies. This is going to be an extremely difficult concept to both explain and understand, but I'll give it my best. In your world, excuse me, in your dimension—uh, in your life, have you ever heard of an area of study called quantum physics?"

"I'm vaguely familiar with it, something like the study of very tiny particles. Like just looking at them changes them?" replied Lola, somewhat tentatively.

"Well, yes. It appears to have been discovered in your world as well. Good. There's also a theory in quantum physics called quantum entanglement. It basically states that quantum particles, or quanta, can mirror each other's state at vast distances, and even across other dimensions, instantaneously, or nearly so. It has a less than scientific sounding name, 'spooky action at a distance.'"

Dr. Fernandez paused briefly to allow Lola to digest what he'd told her.

"Wow, that's some freaky sounding stuff. But it's just a theory, right?"

"Actually, laboratory experiments seem to bear out this theory. I know it's hard to believe. Einstein couldn't either. You've heard of him?"

"Oh, yeah. E equals m c squared and all that."

"Yes, so our worlds *are* quite similar. He was spooked by the idea of action beyond the speed of light. Thus, the 'spooky action' label. Now, to expand on that, there are computers that take advantage of the many states that the quanta can be in, versus the on or off of traditional binary computers. Capacities and speeds are greatly accelerated. Now, if you recall, I mentioned a concept called quantum entanglement. One of the new computers suddenly stopped working on the task it was assigned and was suddenly switched to another task altogether, with completely different data storage. Computer scientists were baffled, and just ended up doing a restore from backup. But there are those of us who believe it switched with another such computer in another world."

"Wow," Lola interjected.

"It gets better. Now there's a significant discipline of neuroscience that believes that our very minds are quantum computers. There is no reason to think that they could not pull the same switch. And that's what I think happened to you."

Stunned silence was Lola's initial reaction. Then, "so how does a medical doctor know so much about all this? An oncologist?"

"Because in another world I also studied physics before getting into medical school and specializing in oncology. You see, the same thing happened to me that has happened to you. You and I slipped and slid, as we have come to call it. I. My entanglement twin in this world had gone on to become a physics professor at Western Carolina Tech, but I decided not to try to fake my way into that arena, but continue on as an oncologist somewhere."

"That must have been quite a feat to accomplish."

"I had to deal with some shady characters to get a different background established, as Doctor Tomas Fernandez, and no it wasn't easy, or comfortable. But it had to be done and I wasn't doing it for nefarious purposes, which eased my conscience. That's not my actual name, which is no longer important. Luckily, my so-called twin in this world, had no family, so his 'disappearance' was only strongly felt by his university colleagues."

"So, you mentioned the word switch?"

"Yes. I must assume that the physicist suddenly found himself in the middle of an oncology conference in my world. That haunts me still, what he must have gone through, is still going through."

"You keep using the term 'world' or 'worlds'," said Lola, more of a question than a statement.

"Yes, you see, the universe is infinite. In it there exists all possible combinations of worlds, usually referred to as dimensions. There's one somewhere where your mind resided, and another for me. When swaps occur, they tend to be between nearly identical worlds. There may even be swaps between identical worlds, but who would know? And they're swaps between DNA-identical people—your doppelganger."

"So, if you're correct, my family and friends must think they're dealing with a mad woman now," said Lola, her voice trailing off at the end. Her thoughts went to wondering how Mick would react. She and he seemed to be hitting it off pretty well after a couple of dates. *Oh well, he'll probably be moving on,* Lola thought.

"As I said, it can weigh on one. But I can help a bit at this end, I think." Dr. Fernandez reached into his briefcase and pulled out some papers. "I basically had a background check run on you, here in this world. I need you to read up on your 'biography' and memorize it. Try to assume this new role. Your attending physician, Dr. Graves should see that you have had a spontaneous recovery from the 'delusions' under which you have been suffering. Once released from this hospital, we can discuss next steps."

"O.K., I think you're getting a little head of yourself here, assuming I believe all this. Maybe I'll just let Dr. Graves know that there's a doctor in this hospital that is as delusional as I am, maybe more. Huh?"

"Maybe. I'm betting you won't, of course. You don't really think you're delusional, do you?"

"I don't know what to think at this point," said Lola with a sigh. "Am I a traditional wacko, or the victim of some cosmic switched at middle age mix-up? By the way, two employees from SolAir dropped by for a visit today. They got here really fast. Damage control, I guess."

"Oh? How did that go?"

"You know, we miss you at SolAir. Hope you can get back into the cockpit real soon. If there's anything we can do for you... Blah, blah, blah. I imagine after yesterday I won't be getting back into a SolAir cockpit, or any cockpit. Wait. What am I saying? I don't belong there anyway."

"We'll cross that bridge when and if necessary."

"Well, let's see my other supposed background."

Dr. Fernandez handed her the papers.

After a few minutes of silent reading, Lola spoke up, "Well, so according to this, I—that is the me that I am now—or whatever, was born in the same place, Fordesboro, NC, at the same date. But the current date is almost five months earlier than I remember. God, this is just so..."

"Yes, it is. So..."

"So, I have also time travelled? I'm nearly five months younger? Doesn't feel much different."

"No. There's no such thing as time travel, because there's no such thing as time. It's a construct we use to measure differences in movement between two objects. For instance, comparing the movement of a person around a track to the movement of a watch, or the aging of the body to the movement of the earth around the sun. There is no travel possible in a concept. But let's go so far as to say time travel *was* possible. Let's say I go back in time only 25 minutes. Unless I take the entire earth with me, I end up where the earth was 25 minutes ago, in the complete vacuum of space. Not a good destination. In only half of that time, I'm probably somewhere near the center of the earth. Again, a sub-optimal outcome. The only science fiction vehicle that I know of that has addressed that issue is *Dr. Who.* The TARDIS on that show stands for Time *and* Relative Distance."

"Oh yeah, great show. Blue police call box, bigger on the inside. What do you think of that concept?"

"Oh, I suppose it's quite possible. Consider that when you enter the confines of the TARDIS, you may slip into another dimension, one where it's actually larger. When you get out, you're in a dimension where it's call box size. But back to the issue of time, other worlds have progressed along other timelines compared to ours. Thus, the time difference. Most of we sliders came from a time-matching or past-shifted world. Though our timeline shifts, those outside of our own sphere of influence tend to match our previous world. Some, like you, will re-live some external events, since you came from a future shifted world. Although your own life is obviously a bit different. Sort of a continuous *déjà vu* of news. I just had a bit of a lost time experience when I slipped in from a slightly past shifted world. So back to *This Is Your Life*."

"I've heard of that show. Our lives, my lives? They seem to pretty much parallel each other until she, or I—so hard to describe—enrolled in flight school. The me I remember went to UNC Fordesboro business school, dropping out in my senior year, doing odd jobs and day-trading in stocks. Got pretty good at retail trading. Was planning on retiring early. I stayed in Fordesboro, the pilot me graduated, trained to be a commercial pilot, and moved to Charlotte. Makes sense, it is a hub airport."

Lola shuffled ahead to the next page and appeared to reread a few lines several times. Then her lips began to quiver and teardrops formed.

"I think I know the part you're reading now," said the Doctor.

After clearing her throat, she managed to choke out the words, "This me has an ex-husband D'Shaun Taylor, and a child, Jadon, in the fourth grade now. He has total custody, along with his current wife, Caitlin. So, I kept my maiden name after the divorce. I'm guessing it was not amicable. I never got married or had a child." At that, Lola put the papers down beside her and took a deep breath. "There's something I haven't told you about yet. I just had a hard time accepting it. This," said Lola, lifting up her hospital gown to reveal a horizontal six-inch scar just below her waistline. Clearly it was a C-section scar.

"So, I guess I'm convinced. I'm not crazy, the universe is," said Lola, lowering her gown. "I'd better get to studying *my* bio, so I can convince the good Dr. Graves that I don't need to be committed, at least not yet. Coming to grips with all this may yet send me over the edge."

"It's been an exciting day. I'll go now. I'll come back tomorrow to check in on you again."

"O.K. Thank you doctor."

Lola wasn't completely convinced, there still lingered a hint of a doubt in her mind of Dr. Fernandez's explanation. But with the alternative being that she was suffering from some mental disease, she was actually grateful for an alternative in which to believe. She got down to reading and memorizing the biography that the doctor had compiled for her. *This life seems so much more interesting,* she thought.

THREE

Lola Gets Her Mind Right

The next day Dr. Graves paid a visit to Lola. She had planned on delving more thoroughly into what might just possibly be a case of multiple identities. Much as with UFOs and ghosts however, exceptional illnesses require exceptional evidence.

"Good morning, Lola. How are you feeling today?"

"Better, actually."

"Oh good. Now, about your memories of your…"

"I'm glad you brought that up," interrupted Lola. "It all has started to come back to me now. My actual past that is."

"And your actual past is?"

"Oh, the one where I'm an air transport pilot, of course."

"Ah," Dr. Graves said, in a flat voice. Then quickly, "that's good. Seems like you're making quick progress. Sometimes there is an immediate recovery."

"Yeah, it just all comes back to me now. Don't know where the other so-called memories came from."

"The mind can make up memories to replace the memory of some trauma that is too hard to recall. Do you know what that might be now?"

"No, nothing really hits me as being so bad I wouldn't want to remember it."

"Well, I suggest regular visits with a doctor who specializes in this area, to maybe work that out."

"You mean a psychiatrist?"

"Well yes. That doesn't necessarily have to have a bad connotation, you know. You're not insane."

"It's just that—you know."

"Yes, I know. But I hope you follow up."

Lola spent the next fifteen minutes relating what she had read about herself in the pages that Dr. Fernandez had provided. Afterwards, Dr. Graves said, "well, you'll likely be getting out of here today. I'll provide a referral for your follow-up visits. Good day."

Dr. Fernandez stepped out of the elevator on the fourth floor and ran into Dr. Graves just coming out of room 412.

"Dr. Fernandez, you seem to have taken quite an interest in my patient. I'd still like to get together and talk about the similar case you had experience with, but our Ms. Sandborne seems to be recovering from her delusions very quickly. One might even say spontaneously. You wouldn't have anything to do with that, would you?"

"Me? No, she doesn't have cancer, as far as I know, so not my area of expertise. I'm just curious. So, I'm glad to hear she's recovering so well."

"Yes, as a matter of fact, she'll be discharged a bit later."

"Glad to hear it. Well, good day Dr. Graves."

"Good day, Doctor."

Dr. Fernandez entered room 412 to see Lola getting dressed in her SolAir uniform.

"I'm getting discharged today."

"Yes, I know. Dr. Graves told me."

"Baby steps. I have to take on this alter ego now."

"I know some people that helped me cope, they should be able to offer some aid to you as well. You see, you and I aren't the only slip sliders around. As a matter of fact, we have a club, of sorts. Simply called the Slip Sliders Club, SSC. Once you get out of here, I'll introduce you to them."

"Must be a very exclusive club."

"It's pretty small, but growing. As more of us are recognized for what we are, and not the 'traditional wackos' you spoke of, it allows us to recognize the same in others. We even have a scientist who is deeply involved in studying the phenomenon, and even attempting to come up with a way to reverse the slide."

"Really? It might be reversible?"

"It may. You see, we actually have a member who slid to another world and returned. He had slipped and slid to a near-world, a near-dimension, that was quite a bit more advanced along its timeline. His condition was recognized there, and it turned out they had determined what caused it, and had developed a method and a technology to reverse it."

"Great! Then we just have to recreate the same technology here," said Lola, the first smile in a few days appearing on her face.

"Well… That's not going to be a simple matter. Remember, the only documentation that could come back with him was his memory itself. Although he spent nearly a year learning as much as he could about the machinery before homesickness overcame him and he decided to head back, we were not sure if he was able to remember enough to reproduce it. He, and the scientist I mentioned, a college professor, are working with a hypnotist to try to recover and document those memories. They are really close. The only thing I know is that it involves a particle accelerator."

"But if it can be pulled off, that would be so great. You could return to your 'normal' life and practice."

"For me, for most of us, it's been too long for that to be practical, or fair for our slip slider partner in the world from which we came. We have to assume they have conformed to the lives we lived, and become accustomed to them, and wouldn't necessarily wish to switch back this far down that road. But maybe, just maybe we can be ready soon enough to flip your switch, so to speak. There's a slim chance."

"I see. Makes sense."

"Just let me know when you're ready to meet them. Mostly it'll be video conferencing, since we're fairly spread out. But the research work is being done near Raleigh."

"You know, I think I'm first going to head to 'my' place in Charlotte, to see what I can find there."

"Sure. Here's my number. Call when you're ready to get together with the club, our slip slider support group."

"Alright. Hopefully I can figure out how to access this mobile, or I may have to get another. It kind of feels criminal, trying to get into 'her' phone, until I realize that I am 'her' now."

"Yes, you are. I guess you shouldn't have any trouble getting home, with your SolAir credentials and uniform."

"Yeah, I just hope no one recognizes me, I'll have no clue who they are," replied Lola with a faint smile.

"Good luck. Let me know how you're doing there, and let me know if you run into any trouble, need any help."

"I will."

Dr. Fernandez got up and left room 412. He had rounds to make.

An hour later, Lola was being discharged. She called for a taxi to show up at the portico outside the main entrance shortly. She was grateful that she was not made to be pushed in a wheelchair during the trip outside to wait for the taxi. She carried her luggage that the one paramedic had brought in. She had never opened it.

A large sedan pulled up to collect Lola. It showed signs of traffic battles lost. The name of the company on the side was an anachronism, chosen to cause it to appear in the first page of the now nearly defunct yellow pages of a telephone directory. She got in, asked the driver to recommend a medium-priced hotel near the airport, recognized the chain name, and told him to head there.

She found the scenery on the ride to the airport up the interstate highway, to be flat and uninteresting, consisting mostly of neatly spaced rows of pine trees. Tree farms, growing wood to satisfy Florida's ever-increasing demand for two by fours, or perhaps, to be made into paper goods. Traffic was light on the six lane road, and the trip brief. It was mostly quiet as well, except for some trivia from the driver. "You know Jacksonville is the largest city in the world, in square miles? The city limits extend as far as the county lines."

"Interesting."

Lola knew she had enough cash to pay for the taxi, but also knew she would be unable to get more, having no knowledge of the PIN code for her ATM card. She reached for a VISA card instead. *Please don't be declined,* she thought. It wasn't. She breathed a slight sigh of relief, and gave the driver a cash tip, thinking that to be preferred. It seemed to be, as he offered to carry her bag in for her. She took it herself, but thanked him for the offer.

Lola approached the front desk and spoke to the clerk on duty. "One room please, for one night."

"Certainly. You can have room 112, at the SolAir discount rate."

Lola handed her the credit card that worked with the taxi. The clerk handed her a same size plastic card as well as returning her VISA card.

"Breakfast is served at seven through ten-thirty."

"Thank you."

Lola found room 112 and inserted the plastic key card into the electronic door lock. She was welcomed with a metallic click and a green light. Inside, she took off her uniform jacket and hung it over the back of a chair. Sitting on the edge of the bed, she took her first look inside of her bag. There was her cap, another white SolAir issued shirt, navy blue uniform pants, and some civilian clothes and extra underwear and socks.

Might ease things along if I just keep wearing the uniform.

But Lola decided to get into the jeans and blouse until the next day. Having done that, she headed toward the hotel business center and looked up SolAir's employee contact information. Back at her room, she sat on the bed once again and picked up the room phone. She was going to have to charge the call to her room, since she couldn't unlock the smart phone. She called the SolAir employee representative.

"SolAir. This is Varsha. How can I help you?"

"Hi. I'm First Officer Lola Sandborne. I'm here in Jacksonville, and I was wondering if you could get me on a flight to Charlotte, hopefully tomorrow."

"Which Jacksonville is that?"

Lola hadn't thought there might be more than one with an airport.

"Uh, Florida."

"Hold for just a moment, please."

Lola waited, gazing about the room at the wall hangings. They all seemed to be aviation related photographs, both current and historic.

"Yes, Lola?" said Varsha, coming back to the phone.

"I'm here."

"I can get you in a cockpit jump seat on a flight tomorrow. How's that?"

Lola thought for a few seconds. *Oh yeah, those stadium-like seats the attendants sit in.*

"Great. Now, I should explain that I'm having memory issues right now. Obviously I'm off of flight duty. This may be a strange question but, do I just show my ID at security and the gate?"

"Well, since you'll be in a jump seat, we prefer you be in uniform as well, but yes. Show your SolAir and another picture ID. You know, driver's license."

"O.K. Thanks." Lola listened intently as Varsha read off the flight number and time of departure. She scribbled it down with the hotel pen and pad, then tore off the sheet and put it in her pocket. "Thanks again. Bye." She went out to try a nearby restaurant, ate dinner and returned to her room. After laying out her uniform and repacking her casual clothes, she dove into bed and quickly dozed off.

Lola awoke without an alarm the next morning. It was eight-thirty. She had plenty of time to have breakfast and catch the hotel shuttle to the airport for a midday flight. She put on her uniform and carried the bag out of the room with her to the breakfast area. She did not anticipate returning to the room.

After breakfast she turned in her plastic key card, caught the shuttle to the airport, and went to security, choosing the line for flight crews. No issues there. On the terminal side, she checked the board for her flight and saw it was on time. She stopped in a nearby newsstand, bought a copy of *The Wall Street Journal*, and went next door to sit and read with a coffee.

A couple of SolAir pilots strode by. One called out to Lola. "Lola, you flyin' today?"

"Uh, no. Dead headin'."

"Oh. See ya."

He turned to his companion and said, "that was odd. Acted like she didn't even know me."

"I don't think she did. Scuttlebutt is she has amnesia—or something.

"Oh, that's sad."

"Yep."

Twenty minutes later, with her plane at the gate, she boarded early, announced herself to the cabin crew, and was shown to the jump seat in the cockpit. She was relieved to not be recognized by anyone else, and in forty-five minutes, she was getting a second row view of the flight that few get to see in person. It was enjoyable watching and listening. Neither of the pilots spoke to her during the flight, which was fine with her.

Lola arrived at Charlotte International that afternoon. Having found an automobile insurance card in her wallet, and a Nissan key fob and a parking ticket in her purse, she knew she had to find a six-year-old Nissan Altima somewhere in the long-term lot. She stepped out of the arrivals area into the brisk autumn air. *I get to experience this fall in North Carolina all over again,* she thought. *My sliding other will be landing right smack dab into a pandemic. Try not to dwell on that, please.*

Lola serpentined around the parking lot, clicking the key fob and listening for a response to her call. Some people stopped and stared for a while, possibly considering if they could help her, then hustling off to catch their flight, or hurrying to get home to family, friends, and jobs. She was making pretty good time, thankful that it was not a hot, humid summer day. After about 15 minutes of walking and clicking, she heard a response. She clicked again to verify that she caused it, and began to home in on the car's location.

The car had the cluttered look of someone always in too much of a hurry to get going, or to get out, to ever tidy up. Her car in the other world was kept tidy and clean. Working from home most of the time, she didn't do much driving. The airline pilot her was always on the go. It started fairly easily and she headed to the exit gate to pay. *Since I don't have a working cellphone, I probably should stop and pick up a map of Charlotte*, she thought. *Should have looked in the airport for one.* She paid and pulled out onto the airport access road.

Lola followed the signs to the interstate ring road. Unsure of which way to go, she moved onto the northerly on ramp, as it was the easiest to access. Two exits later she pulled off and found a convenience store.

"Sorry ma'am, we don't sell maps anymore. There's a large bookstore in towards town that probably sells local maps," said the clerk, pointing in the direction to travel.

Lola left and headed towards town, scanning for the bookstore. She found it, and they did carry a city map. Lola bought it and a highlighter. She sat down at their coffee shop table to study it, marking the way to the address listed on her driver's license. She then headed back out to the car. She spread the map out on the passenger seat, and was on her way to find what would be her new home.

The location of the one-bedroom apartment told Lola she was either not being very well paid as a first officer, or just wasn't home enough to justify larger, more luxurious quarters, or probably a combination of the two.

Locating the apartment, she parked close and sat for a while, working up the nerve to head to the second floor and go on in. *If someone recognizes you, just smile and wave*, Lola cautioned herself.

Steeling herself for the reveal, Lola climbed the stairs to apartment 206, and stood at the door. Selecting a key that looked like it should be the one to the door, she inserted it. It fit. She turned it, and peered inside. *Am I prepared to find out what I've been up to? Will I be disappointed if I haven't been up to much of anything?*

"Honey, I'm home," she said jokingly, in an attempt to lower her apprehension. "Hope you're not," she added. All was quiet   inside.   Lola   was   home.

FOUR

Who is Lola When She's at Home?

The first priority was to see what provisions there were. Checking the refrigerator, Lola determined that her twin must eat out a lot. *Just like an amnesia victim re-learning her life,* Lola thought. There were mostly drinks, some condiments and jellies, some were well out of date. The freezer held mostly ice and some microwave dinners. Lola started a mental grocery list. A sign on a cabinet door caught her attention:

Check ingredients for peanuts!

The living room and dining room were one open space, on the other side of a kitchen pass through. It was sparsely furnished. Just by the pass through there was a small breakfast-nook sized rectangular table and chairs. In the living room section, there were a recliner and love seat, both covered in synthetic leather, an entertainment center against the far wall, a small bookcase against a side wall. On the other side wall, to the bedrooms side, was a small desk with two drawers and a laptop computer on top. The floors were a gray vinyl with a pattern that resembled wood flooring. The walls were all an off-white color. She dropped her purse on the table and headed toward the bookcase.

I wonder what I've been reading, thought Lola as she scanned the book titles. Suspense novels predominated. The only non-fiction Lola saw on the shelves were manuals that pertained to the type of aircraft she had suddenly found herself in. *Read it, read it, oh not that one,* she thought, working her way up from the bottom shelf. *Definitely not this one,* she thought, as she spotted a book on sports betting lying on top of the bookcase. Picking it up, she opened it to where it was bookmarked and saw that it was a chapter on football betting. The bookmark was a slip of paper with the notation:

Pascal: San Francisco and points (vs Carolina) 5k

Wow, that is so not me, thought Lola immediately, then: *oh wait, I basically place bets on stocks all day long. So it* is *me. Did I win? Lose? Has the game not been played yet? Is Pascal a person or a web site?* Lola closed the book and replaced it on the shelf. She retraced her steps back into the opening for the kitchen, turned left into the bedroom. The door was open.

There was a double bed centered against the far wall, with a night table on the left side, as seen looking in from the small entryway where she stood. The bed was made neatly, but without any flourishes. On the right side, a small chest of drawers was against the wall. A closet took up the rest of the room, just to her right, extending from the entryway wall to her right to the rightmost wall. She faced the closet and slid the door so the left side opened up. Hanging inside were a couple of SolAir uniforms like the one she still had on, a few pair of blue jeans, and half a dozen blouses. Lola got out of her uniform, tossed it on the bed, and tried on a pair of jeans and a purple blouse. *Good fit,* she thought, checking her looks in a full-length mirror on the outer right half door of the closet. Lola got out of her dress shoes and tried on a pair of athletic shoes found in the bottom of the closet, next to a pair of what looked like hiking boots. They were a good fit as well. *Just make yourself at home,* thought Lola. *Right, this is home now.*

Feeling more comfortable now, Lola retraced her steps and sat down at the desk in the living room. She booted up the laptop. It asked her for her password and provided a small entry window. She used the wireless mouse to select the beginning of the window and paused, watching it blink. "Now, what would I pick as a password?" Lola said out loud to herself. A framed school picture of a young mixed-race child sat on the corner of the desk, "You must be Jadon. I'm your new mother." Focusing back on the task of gaining entry to the computer, Lola again spoke out loud, "Could it be possible that…" On a hunch, Lola picked up the mouse and flipped over the cushioned pad it rode on. *"Voila!"* said Lola as she spied the writing on the back. Several lines were written and struck through, leaving:

Wildbluey0nd3r

Not bad, but left in a bad place, Lola thought, as the computer accepted her entry. *Now let's see if we can check on finances.*

Lola went to where she normally securely stored her user-ids and passwords. *Thank God it's the same type of computer,* she thought. After gaining access to e-mail, she culled out the ones trying to sell her something, which was the vast majority, and read the one from SolAir.

SolAir sends its regrets for your recent medical incident. Based on the information
provided to SolAir, your current fit for flight duty status must be considered: unfit.
Please make an appointment at your earliest convenience with an AME to determine:
    a: That you should be placed on short term disability.
    b: That you can be returned to flight duty.
    c: Other.
Until such time, you may draw pay from your sick bank until the above has been completed, or the bank has been depleted.

Regards;
John Teschedi,
Human Resources Senior Analyst

I'm pretty sure I don't want: "other," thought Lola.

Before Lola could move on and try to determine her fiscal status, her concentration was interrupted by a knock on the apartment door. She thought for a moment about just ignoring it, but then decided that trying to hide was not going to help her. She got up and walked slowly to the door, her heartbeat increasing. Lola paused, then the knock was repeated. *O.K., time to face my fears. O.K., more of my fears,* she thought.

She opened the door to see a woman standing there, smiling. She was a quite attractive brunette, seemingly younger than Lola, and well dressed. "Lola, how was your last flight?" she asked, cheerfully.

"Uh, there was an issue," replied Lola.

"Oh, I'm sorry. Some sort of in-flight emergency? I hear passengers are behaving frightfully lately."

"Uh, more of a personal issue. What's up," asked Lola, trying to sound nonchalant.

"Well, it looks like you parked in the space that Eric claims as his, and you know how he gets, you know?"

"Actually, I don't. You see, that's the issue. I've suddenly had problems with memory. Really, really, bad problems with memory. As a matter of fact, I don't know who you are. I'm sorry. I hope you can understand."

"Oh, my. That is terrible. Uh, I'm Rita. Rita Van Trop, the neighbor downstairs. Uh, you really don't remember? We went hiking together a few weeks ago."

"No, I'm sorry, I don't. I've been flying airplanes for over ten years now, as I understand it, and I can't remember how to do that. That's where I am right now."

"Wow. I was going to ask when you were free to go hiking with me again. I was thinking about hikes in the forest," said Rita, with clearly a look of concern on her face.

Apparently, we are friends? Lola thought. "That sounds good, actually. And as luck would have it, I won't be flying anytime soon, maybe never again. I'm available whenever."

"Great, so I'll give you a call when I can work it out," said Rita.

"Well, maybe you should just come up here again," Lola said. "You see, I'm still trying to remember how to get into my cell phone."

"Oh. Sure."

"So, where should I move my car? You know, so as not to antagonize Eric?" asked Lola.

"Well, you know what, it would do him good to realize we don't have assigned spaces. But if you don't mind, just move one space to the right. To avoid unpleasantries. Well, good night. I'll see you later. Take good care of yourself, please get better, and if you need anything, just call. I'm sorry, if you need anything just come down to 106," said Rita.

"Sure thing. Thank you so much."

When Rita left, Lola went and moved her car one space to the right. She suddenly felt less alone in this world.

Back in the apartment, she bent to the task of gaining access to her cellular telephone. It must have been recently updated or turned off or the other Lola had not enabled biometrics. It demanded a number. Lola had already tried a passcode of her later birthday in this world, tried it month, day, year; day, year month; with two-digit and four-digit year, to no avail. She wondered how many attempts were left before all was lost. Then it occurred to her. She went back to the kitchen table and pulled Dr. Fernandez's papers out of her purse. There was Jadon's birthday. On the second try, month, day, four-digit year, the phone revealed itself to her. Checking voicemails, there were two from the person listed in her contacts as Pascal. She listened in to the last one.

"Lola, what's going on. It's very important you talk to me. I haven't been able to get ahold of you for several days now. I really need that money. Call, damn it."

Again, a feeling of fear came over Lola. This guy sounds serious. *What the hell have I been up to?* Again, she considered just ignoring this new information she had discovered. But what if that would place her life in danger? She called back.

There was a near immediate answer, "Lola, what is going on? These guys are serious. I really need to get them some money and soon. I thought we had a deal?"

"Well, this may be hard to believe, but I've had some issues with my memory," replied Lola.

"How convenient. But seriously, I still owe over 4k to these guys. And they play for keeps.".

"Look, I'll get you what I can as soon as I can. But I'm serious too. I found a bet written down, but for the life of me, I can't remember making it. By the way, why do you call yourself Pascal?"

"Huh? Because—that's my name?"

"Oh. I kind of thought, maybe people involved with this kind of thing would use pseudonyms. You know, the famous mathematician."

"Well maybe, but we go back to high school, you and I. That's why I gave you a break on this loss. Carried it on my own book. But now 'they' are comin' a callin'. You *really* don't remember, do you?"

"No, I don't. I'm having to relearn everything," replied Lola. "I need to better understand my own financial sitch, then I'll call you back, I promise."

"You better. Don't let me down."

Well, I guess that bet didn't pan out, Lola thought. *Oh yeah, come to think of it, I remember that was a bit of an unexpected road win for Carolina.*

A germ of an idea began to form in her mind, then Lola realized she was feeling a bit hungry. She found some snack crackers in a kitchen cabinet and munched on those, while formulating a plan. Then for the first time in several days, she found herself relaxed enough to finally start feeling sleepy.

Lola wrestled over whether or not she was up to spending the night in the apartment, sleeping in a strange bed. She decided eventually that there was no sense in putting it off. She stripped to her underwear and crawled into bed for the first night in her new home. With suddenly nothing to do to occupy her mind, she began to think of just how unreal the past four days had been. Here she was, taking over someone's life, without any memory of what came before, just basically the same knowledge as what a prospective employer would find out before hiring. To top it all off, the same thing was happening to her counterpart in another world. *She likely would know even less about my life up until four days ago,* thought Lola. *Apparently, neither of us Lolas kept any kind of a journal or diary.*

She finally managed to quiesce the thoughts that were causing her so much turmoil. She switched to thinking about taking advantage of the knowledge of future events external to her life. Also calming was the thought that for at least a while, she had a refuge from having to lie about not remembering her life. She could remember all of her previous life, including five months yet to occur, that she was free to modify. They just weren't the same memories those who knew her in this world had of her. Lola finally slipped into unconsciousness.

FIVE

Welcome to the Club

Lola awoke the next morning well after sunrise, after a particularly vexing dream. In it, she had gone back to college to finish her degree. This time around, she was unable to make any friends, much less any romantic attachments. Not that she had a serious boyfriend at the time she slid either, though Mick seemed promising. Even though she was sure she was back at UNC Fordesboro, the campus was totally unfamiliar to her. Just before she awoke, she realized in her dream that she had not completed any classwork for weeks, suddenly rushing about in a panic that she was so far behind, and unable to find a classroom, time running out to attend. "Not again!" she tried to scream, but nothing came out.

Bolting upright after the vivid dream, Lola climbed out of bed, dressed, and went into the kitchen, hoping to find coffee and a maker. *Oh, good,* she thought as she spied the drip coffee maker, and found some ground dark roast in a cabinet. *My favorite.* Recalling that there was no breakfast meat, or any eggs, she settled for a couple of toaster pastries to eat.

Lola had managed the previous day to gain access to her on-line banking by resetting that password through e-mail. That password had not been stored with the others. She found that there was precious little money available to her, and her credit was stretched pretty thin. It was nearly a week until the next paycheck arrived. Lola had set up an on-line brokerage account that remained unfunded. She decided that it was time to take up Dr. Fernandez's offer of help. Sitting at the table having her breakfast, she dialed his number on her newly freed-up phone. Now all she had to do was look at it. As expected of a busy doctor, her call went to voicemail.

"Good morning, Dr. Fernandez. This is Lola; Lola Sandborne. I've gotten settled in as best I can here in Charlotte, but… Uh, I recall you offering to help if you could, and mentioning a support group of sorts, the Slip Sliders Club? I'd like to learn more about them if I could. Please call me back at…" Lola said, and hung up the phone.

While she waited for Dr. Fernandez to return her call, Lola delved deeper into text message history. She found the most recent text message from D'Shaun Taylor. It said, *Lola, you missed your last visitation appointment. Jadon was really hurt. He still looks forward to your visits. After all, you are still his mother. Are you O.K.?* The message was over two weeks old, and no response had been sent. Lola grappled with the decision of whether to do a deeper dive into this alternate life, or to maintain a distance, with the hope that she could soon be returned to her familiar one.

She began to wonder what caused pilot Lola to not show up. *Let's see what's going on with her?* She dug deeper into e-mail history: a month previous to the most recent e-mail. *Lola, Jadon enjoyed the trip to the zoo with you, but I'm concerned about what he told me. He said you told him that you were his mommy, but he has a new mommy now, and that she should take over completely. He considers you both his mother. I'm a bit concerned.*

What changed? Thought Lola. *Is it the gambling and the one degree of separation from some sketchy characters? Maybe she's trying to protect them?*

Just then, her cell phone rang. "Hello?"

"Lola, this is Dr. Fernandez, I've got a few minutes to talk. I'm so glad to hear you've settled in, at least somewhat, to your new circumstances. I'm really very impressed with your progress so far. Before, I've gotten panicked calls much sooner. So yes, it's time you met the members of Slip Sliders Club. I'll set up an on-line meeting for six o'clock tonight, eastern time. So, you do have access to a computer now, I assume?"

"Yes, I do."

Dr. Fernandez continued with the details of how to log in to the video meeting, and finished with the phrase he always used with new members, "You are not alone."

"Thank you, Dr. Fernandez. I don't know what I would have done without you," before realizing that Dr. Fernandez likely did not have someone like himself assisting him, yet somehow survived his slipping and sliding into this world, this dimension, as it were. Survived, thrived, and still had the altruism to help others, as with his chosen profession. They both terminated the conversation.

Lola spent a few hours exploring more of the apartment. There were photos found of her and D'Shaun and Jadon, obviously in happier times. She peered at one particular photo of the three of them in the Great Smoky Mountains National Park, in front of a waterfall, smiling as if the rest of the world did not matter. *How could she leave this life behind?* wondered Lola. Eventually she would get her answer to that question. *I wish I could have had it.*

Lola got back on the computer and looked up the record of the Carolina Panthers professional football team. Suddenly it hit her. *They didn't win another game the rest of the season. I remember that. Eight losses in a row. It was big news, their catastrophic collapse.* Part of the plan she had been formulating in her mind, suddenly gelled completely. This, and the other part of her plan, already burned into her brain, depended upon gaining funding. *I've got the knowledge to get rich, but so little seed money,* thought Lola.

Lola spent the rest of the day shopping for groceries, making lunch, and wondering what she would learn from the meeting with the Slip Sliders Club. She was filled with hope for the first time in quite a few days. As she sat at home having lunch, thoughts of D'Shaun and Jadon intruded. Pulling back up the latest text message from D'Shaun, she began to formulate a response.

I'm sorry I missed the last visit with Jadon. You see, I'm having issues with my memory. Right now, I'm on leave from the airline. I'm not sure if I'll ever be back flying again. It's really a stressful time. I hope you can understand. I really would like to see Jadon again. Please let me know when that can be arranged. I hope you can allow some indulgence for my current condition. Lola.

She hesitated briefly, then sent the message on its way.

Lola took an afternoon nap. The circumstances of the previous days had taken a toll on her mind and body. At 4:30, she awoke and began looking forward to the meeting with the SSC.

Dr. Fernandez contacted a fellow slider, who also happened to be a medical doctor, an epidemiologist as a matter of fact. He had e-mailed out a general notice concerning a new Slip Slider member, and the scheduled special meeting, and followed up with text messages and voice mails urging them to check their e-mail for an important announcement. There was however, a matter he felt would be of special importance to member Ricky Chan, MD.

Dr. Chan was a slip slider who had come from a nearly identical world. One day he suddenly had about two hours of time he could not account for. He wondered if he may have been a victim of an alien abduction, but dismissed those as mere legend. Then he began to notice subtle differences around him. Studies he knew that had been done were no longer available. Then there were not so subtle differences. For instance, a colleague that he had spoken to weeks before, suddenly did not exist.

He considered consulting a psychiatrist. Then, one day while doing an internet search on his symptoms, a reference to slip sliders came up. It mentioned the Slip Sliders Club and Dr. Fernandez, with whom he attempted to correspond.

Dr. Fernandez, being careful of his reputation in the oncology community, carefully vetted Dr. Chan's case before responding to his entreaties. Becoming convinced of his authenticity, Dr. Fernandez explained what had he was sure had occurred, and welcomed him to the club. They become frequent correspondents. Dr. Fernandez eventually convinced Dr. Chan to immigrate to America, which was made easier by his professional standing. He settled in Seattle, Washington.

"Good afternoon, Doctor Chan, Doctor Fernandez here. How are you this afternoon?"

"Doing well, Doctor. I hope you are as well. I understand we have a new member of our little club."

"Yes. I wanted to give you some more details about her qualification for membership. They may be of interest to an epidemiologist such as yourself. When I first met Lola, she was expressing surprise that no one on the airplane she found herself in, no one in the hospital as well, was wearing a mask."

"A mask?"

"Yes. She is from a time-shifted world, approximately five months farther along than ours. She mentioned a pandemic, COVID-19, and a mask order. Given her comments, I am concerned that within five months from now we will be experiencing a public health emergency, a pandemic, if not an epidemic," said Dr. Fernandez. "Unless prophylactic action can be taken. By the way, I haven't yet mentioned her time delta to the rest of the members."

"COVID-19? I suppose it could mean a coronavirus, COV. Nineteen for the year? They cause the common cold, and can cause more severe diseases such as SARS, as has ravaged through cruise ships," said Dr. Chan. "But a version that calls for masking of the population? I can't see that," he added.

"Still, I would like to keep Lola, you and I together on the video meeting afterwards, to see if we can flesh out more details about this COVID-19."

"Sure, sure. It's something that should be delved into deeper. But let me ask you, even if Lola experienced a pandemic in her near-world, does that necessarily mean that would happen in ours?"

"I think so. As you know, individuals such as Lola can experience some divergence between her world and ours. Even significant differences can manifest. However, overall, events that are affected by groups of people tend to match between most slip slider near-worlds. I refer you to the case of Ronaldo DeCantos."

"Yes, wasn't he time-shifted by only three days forward in his previous world?"

"True. But don't you remember what he correctly predicted?"

"Oh yeah. The major Argentine sudden economic downturn."

"Yes. Not so much predicted, as recounted," explained Dr. Fernandez. "Are you familiar with a concept called the wisdom of crowds?" he asked.

"Sure. Something like: a single person's estimate can be very inaccurate, but if many people are queried and their estimates averaged, the average tends very close to the actual value."

"Very good. For instance, a study was conducted that asked people how much an average cow weighs. Estimates, or in some cases, wild guesses, ranged from 300 to 2000 pounds. Yet after a sufficient number of random people were queried, the average was within five percent of the accepted value," said Dr. Fernandez "By the way, how much do you think an average cow weighs?"

"Well, let's see." Dr. Chan was silent for a few seconds, obviously pondering Dr. Fernandez's challenge. He didn't like to not know—anything. "I'll say, One thousand pounds."

"The actual figure is 750 pounds. You were off by twenty-five percent. The 'crowd' was off by five percent. I have a similar theory for near-dimensions. I call it the momentum of crowds. That is, even though individual histories may diverge between near-worlds, they do not affect the histories of groups. So even though Lola's history certainly differs between her old world and the one she finds herself in now, I think the significant history that she has observed in hers, will also occur in ours. I hope that we can find a way to change that."

"I defer to your superior probability and statistics expertise. I guess the question is, should we even try to change that? What else will it change? How?"

"Well, not that there is even a chance we can, but the one thing it would change, is perhaps saving many, many lives. I was sort of looking to you for the how, with your background. Anyway, that's why I want us to interview Lola after the general meeting. O.K.?"

"Sure. 'See' you at the meeting, Dr. Fernandez."

"And afterwards, Dr. Chan. Thank you for your time. Goodbye."

SIX

▨ ▦ △

Meet and Greet

Lola was logged in to the meeting early. Dr. Fernandez had already opened it up to signing in, and was notified when she did.

"Good evening, Lola. How are you doing?" He asked.

"A bit apprehensive. It's always hard for me, meeting people for the first time. I'm usually pretty bad at first impressions."

"Don't worry. Remember, they've all been in your shoes. So, what's going on with your employer?"

"Well obviously I won't be flying again, but they don't know that. So, I get checks from a so-called sick bank, as long as that holds out. Hopefully I can get back on my feet trading stocks before then. I do have that four-plus-month window to use what I remember to my advantage."

"I hope so. By the way, might be best for now to keep the time shift info between us and Dr. Chan for now. Lola, after the meeting ends, and most sign off, please remain logged on. I want you and I to have an after-meeting discussion together with Dr. Ricky Chan."

"About what?"

"Well, remember when we first met, and you were wondering why everyone wasn't wearing masks?"

"Of course,' said Lola, in a voice that was more question than statement.

"And you mentioned that was because of a pandemic, of COVID-19?" continued Dr. Fernandez.

"Yes. That was confusing, although a lot less confusing than suddenly being at the controls of a jet airliner."

"Dr. Ricky Chan, another slider, is an epidemiologist. I would like you to speak with him after the meeting, to see what else you can tell him, and me, about the pandemic. O.K?"

"I'll try to help."

"Very good."

"So, you are the president of the club?"

"De facto, you might say. Being so small, there are only sixteen of us now, we're fairly informal. But I kind of moderate the quarterly meetings and of course send out notifications of any major events, like—well, you."

"For such a small club, seems like there are a preponderance of advanced degreed professionals"

"It does seem that way. Maybe there's a connection somehow between intelligence and tendency toward slipping and sliding, don't know. We are a small sample size. Mostly we are Americans also, a few Europeans, an Aussie, one Chilean and Dr. Chan, our naturalized citizen member from China. Obviously we may never know about cases in more news restrictive countries, and less connected and more distant countries."

Other names and faces began to appear after a few minutes silent wait. "Looks like most everyone has logged on, we'll give Roberta a few minutes," said Dr. Fernandez. After another few, "O.K., looks like Roberta is a no-show, let's get started." He first introduced Lola and explained her situation, minus the time shift part for now, including their encounter in a Florida hospital.

Lola recounted her story, minus the time differential part, and added, "and now I must tell my employer I can't remember how to fly their jets, a friend that I can't remember who they are, as well as an ex-husband and son that I can't recall."

The doctor then introduced the members and gave their backgrounds, including major differences between their current and previous worlds. They then proceeded to tell their stories.

Lola was particularly intrigued by the story of wind turbine technician Todd Longrain, he being the only known round-tripping slip slider to date, and second most recent one. The background in his live feed appeared to be that of a messy motel room, one of the cheaper varieties.

Todd began his story. "I was doing some maintenance on turbines in a Texas wind farm when it happened to me. Surprisingly, Texas, though being known for its oil production, has extensive wind power. Anyway, I suddenly found myself in a garage bay, holding a diagnostic meter attached to an electric car. This was in a car dealership in California; Oxnard. Obviously you all know what an incomprehensible shock that is. At first I thought I must have been tripping on some sort of psychedelic drug or something, maybe someone slipped into my coffee. I had never experimented with such. But then I realized my surroundings were all too real. As usual in those situations I ended up being hospitalized for observation after the manager of the car dealership decided to call emergency services." Todd paused for a moment and cleared his throat. "Sorry, that memory still haunts a bit."

Dr. Fernandez interrupted, giving Todd time to regain his composure. "At this end we were monitoring the news, as we do, for stories like Todd's where he suddenly seemed totally disoriented and shaken up. So much so, he had to be rescued from the top of a wind turbine, where he had supposedly been working comfortably."

Todd jumped back in. "Yeah, my alternate probably had a worse day. I was lucky also in that there was an SSC club and a Dr. Fernandez equivalent in the near-world I slipped into, though that wasn't his name. Another member of their club came to see me in the hospital and told me what she thought had happened. It was really hard to swallow her story at first, but when she told me that in that world, they had figured out how to reverse the process, well then I thought, O.K., show me! Then the doctor showed up and worked on getting me out of the hospital, and arranged the reversal. But first I spent the better part of a year learning as much as I could about the process. I worked with a hypnotist to try to embed the details into my subconscious. Apparently, it worked, they've been able to pry out the info from my mind with the help of a hypnotist where I am, here."

Lola broke in. "I'm really curious about how the switchback works."

At this, Dr. Fernandez took over again. "As I believe I mentioned, it requires the use of a particle accelerator. To force a switch requires a lot of surrounding energy at the sub-atomic level. Todd had to actually stand in the accelerator tunnel while it was running. He wore a specially made suit that protected his body from harm, of course. It wouldn't do to force his alternate self, back into a body riddled by radiation."

"Yeah, that was really freaky. It was like I was dropped into the center of the Sun, it was so bright around me. But eerily quiet. And then I was suddenly back here, also working on an electric car. In Denver."

Dr. Fernandez jumped in again, adding, "Yes, we had worked with the Todd who had slid here, getting him adjusted to his alternate life, and back to his familiar vocation. Hopefully at the other end, he was able to adjust again. That is after getting over the shock of suddenly being in a particle accelerator tunnel while it ran at full blast." This elicited chuckles from the members.

"And then I went back to working the turbines," said Todd. "And working with Professor Gibbons, another member, on sussing out the workings of the reversal process."

"So, this process doesn't require any action at the other end?" asked Lola.

"No, other than they have to still be alive with a sound mind," answered Todd. "So, we need to take into account that it's involuntary on the other end. Weigh possible consequences on both ends."

Dr. Tomas Fernandez continued, "We believe we're close to recreating Todd's experience. The main thing we're lacking is access to the particle accelerator, and we're working on gaining a confederate at one near Raleigh. Lola, you would likely be one of the early candidates to give it a try, if you so desired. The rest of us are pretty set in our current lives, or don't want to involuntarily return our counterparts, except for Roberta. She didn't make this meeting."

"Lola, I'm Professor Ronald Gibbons." She searched for his face on the screen. He was much younger that she expected a professor to look. "I teach engineering courses at Southern Georgia. I'm working on recreating the protective suit you would need to wear, trying to get the protection needed, but without being too heavy and cumbersome. It's basically going to be a wearable Faraday cage, based on the information given to us by Todd. We're getting close."

"Thank you, professor," said Lola.

There was one more story to be told.

"Jon, why don't you go ahead with your experience?" said Dr. Fernandez.

"O.K. Well, I'm a real estate broker. Was in my previous near-world also. My counterpart here was also, and our lives ran so identical that at first, I had not even realized I had slipped. I only felt an odd sensation one day, akin to déjà vu, or having a premonition. Then, odd things began to happen, like a house I was supposed to show suddenly wasn't even on the market, and the occupants looked at me like I had lost my mind. Which I thought I had. Also, a vacant house in a pricy subdivision that had been on the market for nine months, when I went to check to see if the lawn needed mowing or any other maintenance was necessary, I was greeted by a vacant lot. Well, I thought I was being gaslighted and started accusing co-workers. I was eventually fired, and turned to professional help."

"Wow, that must have been freaky," interjected Lola. "Not clearly schizophrenic, but definitely paranoid."

"Are you a medical professional?"

"No. Sorry. Please continue."

"Well, some internet site got wind of the story, put it out there, which one of the slip sliders noticed, and here I am. Of course, it took quite some convincing, but once Dr. Fernandez got involved, I started to believe."

"Yes, he is quite convincing," Lola agreed.

"O.K., I believe that concludes our special meeting of the Slip Sliders Club. Lola, are you fine with joining our next quarterly meeting? It's only about three weeks away. Or do you think you'd like another special one called?" asked Dr. Fernandez.

"No, I'm fine with waiting."

"Excellent. Goodnight, everyone, and thank you so much for participating."

One by one the meeting participants dropped off until only the two doctors and Lola remained.

Dr. Fernandez broke the silence. "Lola, before we get started on the subject that I wished to discuss, there is another matter. I think you will appreciate it. You see, we have established a fund for new slip sliders, that can provide a monthly stipend for you for some time until you have been able to establish yourself in your new world as providing for yourself. We understand this may take quite some time, so the payout is fairly open ended, we just ask that you show some initiative in getting on your feet, so to speak, in this world. I don't think that will be an issue for you, as you have already shown remarkable progress in diving into your counterpart's business. But don't be in any hurry to have us stop payments. O.K.?"

"Oh, how generous. I certainly wouldn't want to abuse such largess."

"Great. Now on to the matter of great importance to Dr. Chan and I. When I first met you, you were concerned that no one around you was wearing a mask. You mentioned a pandemic that you referred to as COVID-19. Can you enlighten us about COVID-19 please? Thanks."

"Oh, sure. It's a virus, one that was traced back to China. It began in a place called Wuhan. Supposedly it was transmitted to humans from bats found in nearby caves, whose meat were sold in so-called wet markets there. Then, there were rumors that a laboratory nearby was enhancing viruses, and that COVID-19 leaked from said laboratory. Anyway, it spread all over the world, and in a hurry. And it was much more deadly than your basic flu virus. Especially to the elderly and those with conditions that weakened the immune system. Millions were projected to die worldwide. The whole world went on lockdown to varying degrees. That's where it stood when I ended up in that airplane cockpit."

"Do you know when it was first noticed? In China, that is?" asked Dr. Chan.

"Sometime in November, 2019. Although it wasn't noticed outside China until early 2020, I think."

"Dr. Chan, don't you know a colleague in Wuhan?" asked Dr. Tomas Fernandez.

"Yes I do. Li Wang. I wonder how much she knows about the studies going on in the Wuhan Institute of Virology?"

"Do you think it's possible to arrange a visit there for us?"

"I'll see, but they are quite secretive."

"So, what are you two on about? Do you think it's possible to shortstop this virus?"

"Chances are low, but we feel compelled to try," answered Dr. Fernandez.

"I will prevent disease whenever I can, for prevention is preferable to cure," said Dr. Chan. "That's in the Hippocratic Oath."

"So, is your passport up to date?" asked Dr. Fernandez.

"Yeah. I guess time is of the essence here," replied Dr. Chan.

"See what you can do to get us a visit to the WIV. Soon. Thanks," said Dr. Fernandez. "Lola, is there anything else you can remember about the virus?"

"Well, the symptoms varied, from a bad cold to basically drowning in fluid. People also mentioned a loss of the sense of taste. That's about all I can remember at the moment. I hope that's helped."

"It's good information. Thanks," said Dr. Chan.

"Well, I think that about wraps up our post-meeting chat. Unless you have anything else you'd like to discuss, Lola," said Dr. Fernandez. "I think we need to contact the Center for Disease Control in Atlanta and see what they know about bats in caves near Wuhan, and what the WIV are studying."

"I'm good for now," said Lola.

"Well, don't hesitate to call me if there's anything else, and good night," said Dr. Fernandez. "Oh wait, you need to give me your banking info and I'll get you your first stipend right away."

"I'll say bye for now," said Dr. Chan, and his video feed disappeared.

After giving the doctor her account information, Lola bid him good night and logged off.

SEVEN

It's Good to be Clairvoyant

The next day early, Lola checked her bank balance again and saw that she was three thousand dollars better off. The plan that she had been formulating could now be put into effect. She picked up the cell phone and dialed Pascal's number.

"Yo."

"Pascal?"

"Who else would it be? This Lola?"

"Uh, yeah. Frankly I didn't expect you to be answering this early. I was fully expecting to leave a voicemail."

"I've got to be up to service my European clientele."

Lola laughed at that comment but Pascal remained silent. *Maybe he's not kidding?*

"So. What's up?"

"I have good news, and a free tip for you."

"Let's have the good news. I can do without the tip."

"O.K. The good news is I can get you two of the five I owe you today. Just tell me where to meet you"

"The usual… Oh yeah, you can't remember. How's about Queen's Grill downtown. At One?"

"Sounds good. What do they have for lunch?"

"People who mind their own business. And a pretty good burger and fries. If you get there first, grab a booth near the back if you can."

Lola thought for a few seconds, then asked, "would you send me a picture so I can recognize you? You know, the memory thing."

"I'll watch for you and wave you over if I get there first. See you then."

Queen's Grill was appropriately run down looking, with the smell of spilled beers and cooking grease in the air. The slight odor of old tobacco smoke seemed to emanate from the walls. *I've been in worse,* thought Lola. *But not much.*

"Sit anywhere you like," came the greeting from the bar.

Where Lola would have liked to sit was at her favorite table at Mama's Place in Fordesboro, for a good home-cooked meal, but just replied, "thanks." She walked slowly to the rear, glancing left and right to try to catch sight of a waving arm. None appeared. She sat down at one of the booths that jutted out from the rear wall and pulled a menu from its holder. After deciding on a grilled cheese and a Coke, she looked around for waitstaff and saw none. Just then a tall lanky man with long blond hair entered the bar and grill, took a few long steps, smiled and waved at Lola.

"Pascal, I presume?" asked Lola.

"'Tis me," Pascal said as he slid down the booth seat across from Lola.

"I must say, you're not what I expected a bookie to look like."

"Good. Did you order yet?"

"No, I haven't seen any wait staff."

"You won't," said Pascal as he pointed to a hand-written sign on the wall next to them.

Please place your order at the bar.
Leave a name.
We'll call you when it's ready.

Thanks,
The Queen

"Ah, I was busy watching for waving man. Missed that, thanks."

"Notice it doesn't say *your* name," said Pascal with a wink. "Ready?"

They both went to the bar and ordered, Lola a grilled cheese and chips with a Coke, Pascal a cheeseburger and crinkle fries, with a **Dr. Pepper**. They sat down with their drinks and Pascal got down to business.

"Don't mean to rush you, but—well, yeah I do actually. You've been avoiding me for about three weeks."

"Oh, here you go," said Lola as she drew out the small bank envelope.

"Good. Only three more large to go, plus the vig."

"About that, I think you want to hear my tip."

"Really? And why's that?"

"Because…" Lola hesitated, working up the courage to go on with a sip of her drink, that was weakening with the melting ice. "Because I know that Carolina is going to lose their last eight games."

"Whaaa? Now let's see. You've lost your memory. But apparently at the same time, you've become, what's that word now, clairvoyant?"

"Exactly! You see, I didn't actually lose my memory, because it's one my mind never had. My mind has seen about five months of your future. So yeah, same reasons."

Pascal broke into loud laughter at that, nearly spewing out the last swallow of his drink. Seeing the glances of the other few patrons, he became silent.

Lola broke the silence with, "I see you'll need a bit of convincing."

"Oh lady, I'll need a whole *shitload* of convincing," said Pascal, again laughing.

"O.K. Let me ask you, how familiar are you with stock markets?"

"Not at all. Stocks are too risky."

"Too risky? For a bookie?"

"I don't usually make bets. That's the risky part. I make money no matter who wins. That's the vigorish part. If I get lopsided with bets on one side or the other, I'll lay some off to balance back to fifty-fifty."

"Oh. Well, I'm quite familiar with stocks, and risk. And I know that tomorrow, on the NASDAQ exchange, a certain stock is going to go down 32 percent. Acurmed is a startup company whose highly touted new drug to treat Alzheimer's has been undergoing a clinical trial. Tomorrow the results of that trial are going to be announced, and to put it mildly, they will be a disappointment. I lost a lot that day."

"I didn't know you dabbled in stocks. And you said *lost,* as in past tense?"

"It's a bit more than dabbling. O.K., here's the thing," said Lola, taking a deep breath before continuing. "I'm not the Lola you knew. Physically yes, but not my mind. I'm from another dimension, a world that's really close to this one, but not quite the same. The two Lola's lives diverged a lot, but not events affected by groups of people. Dr. Fernandez called it the momentum of crowds. And one more thing; my world was ahead by almost five months. I have, what Dr. Fernandez called, slipped and slid into this world."

"Dr. Fernandez? You're from five months in the future? Oh, never mind. Lola, in school I always thought you were one of the more stable people. Are you on drugs? Had a traumatic brain injury?"

"Just take a look at Monday's market. At four o'clock, check the closing price of stock ticker ACMD. If you had some experience with stocks, I would suggest shorting it. I know I'll be on the right side this time. Though I don't have enough money now to make much."

"Shorting?"

"Yeah. You can borrow a stock at its current price, agreeing to pay back the lender before a certain time. Then, you can sell it. Unlike a normal loan, you don't pay back what you borrowed, you pay back what it's worth at some point before payment is past due. Hopefully much lower."

"Sounds good."

"Only if the price goes down. You could end up paying more."

"So maybe you just have some inside information, and you're just having some fun with me."

"Would I have inside information on how much the stock will drop? Give me a call after four Monday. The NASDAQ exchange keeps banker's hours, 9:30 to 4:00."

"Sure. Good to see you again. Pay at the bar on the way out." With that, Pascal got up to leave.

"Oh, Pascal, one more thing. What's your last name?"

"Veranos. It's Spanish for summers. My mother was French though."

"Interesting mix. Catch you tomorrow."

That Monday, at 4:15 p.m., Lola was at what she had accepted as home. Her phone rang. She knew who was on the other end.

"Convinced?" was the greeting Lola blurted out.

"ACMD down 31.7 percent. I gotta say, pretty spooky. You uh, remember any of the game scores, the eight losses? You know, so point spreads come into play."

"No, I really never paid much attention to the games. I just remember them finishing the second half of the season winless."

"O.K., doesn't really matter."

"So, what do you think now about using my tip for an eight-game parlay? Half of what I gave you Saturday for me, take the rest out of my net winnings until I catch up. Whaddya say?"

"Let me think about it. It'll be a game-time decision, as they say. I'll let you know. I mean, they won yesterday."

"O.K., but that was the last time this season. Bye for now, then?"

"Yep. Bye."

Lola hung up, then checked for text messages. There was one from D'Shaun: *Sorry to hear about your memory loss. I understand. Just let me know when you're ready to come visit.* Lola glanced at the photos of her estranged husband and son. A familial longing filled her. She typed out the simple reply, *I'm ready. Say when,* and sent that.

EIGHT

In China it's Just Food

Dr. Fernandez called on Dr. Chan to verify their plans. "So, we meet at the Wuhan Institute of Virology in two days, right? Which is just a day and a half for us. International Dateline, you know."

"Yes, exactly."

"Are you sure you want me to come along? I'm not an epidemiologist like you, you know."

"No, but you're not exactly lacking a medical background. And you excel at strategies, unlike me. You're definitely coming with."

"That's good to hear. The flight I booked is non-refundable."

Dr. Chan chuckled. "You were sure, weren't you?"

"Fairly certain."

"I'm not quite sure what this will accomplish. I've just managed to get a tour of the facilities thanks to my old school chum Dr. Li Wang. I helped her through organic chemistry and some other subjects. At least maybe we can decide if the COVID-19 virus can possibly escape from there and infect the population. If not, then we move on to the nearby caves and the wet market."

"Get lots of rest. The flight, at least in coach, probably violates some of the Geneva Convention. I have a brief layover in San Francisco, which helps a bit. How about you?"

"The same, but I doubt we'll run into each other."

"Yeah, see you there. Call me when you get in."

"Same, same. Bye."

Two exhausted doctors met up for breakfast in a hotel restaurant in Wuhan. Luckily it catered to foreigners, and offered bacon and eggs.

"Good morning, Dr. Chan. Do you think the bacon is safe?"

Dr. Chan let out his signature chuckle and answered, "I think so. It appears to be well cooked. As long as it's not bat bacon."

The two ate, grateful not to have to navigate through a mysterious menu.

"O.K., so we ask if they are investigating coronaviruses transmitted via bats. If not, what do we do?" asked Dr. Chan.

"I've given that some thought. How committed are you to forestalling this pandemic?"

"What exactly do you mean?"

"Are you willing to falsify records? Because I am."

"What?"

"We need to get it across to both Chinese and American authorities that this virus has jumped across to the human population. Because if it already hasn't, it soon will."

"So we fake just such an occurrence?"

"I believe we must."

"Wow. You know, I think you're right. In this case, I think the ends *do* justify the means."

"Ready to meet Dr. Wang?"

"Let's go."

◉ ✕ 🦇

Dr. Wang met the two in the lobby of the WIV, and instructed them in the procedure to enter the level four facility.

"I am so glad to see you again Dr. Chan," Dr. Wang said in Mandarin.

"And I to see you," Dr. Chan replied. "Can we speak in English? Dr. Fernandez does not speak Mandarin."

"Sure. And such a pleasure to meet you, Dr. Fernandez," said Dr. Wang, switching to English.

"Nice to meet you. Your English is excellent," said Dr. Fernandez.

"Now, if you will be kind enough to change into these suits. There is a room just to the right, for this purpose. Thank you so much."

After changing into what was basically a jumpsuit, boots, and headgear, they were required to step into a pool of disinfectant, then into a spray of the same from above. Following Dr. Wang into the facility, they began to ask questions.

Dr. Chan asked, "Dr. Wang, have you a study of certain coronaviruses, particularly those that may have been transmitted from bats that populate caves west of Wuhan?" They felt air pressure decreases in their ears as they went through airlocks to inner rooms.

"We have samples of certain of those coronaviruses, but have not done much study on them as we consider them unlikely to jump to the human population."

Dr. Fernandez interjected, "what if we told you we already have evidence of just such a jump?"

Dr Wang appeared surprised, then asked, "what evidence would that be, Dr. Fernandez?"

"An airline passenger appeared in Seattle, showing symptoms of a coronavirus infection. Coughing, fever, loss of taste especially."

Dr. Chan glanced at him, then nodded.

"Oh, and you think it might be from a local infection?"

"That's what I would like to know. Could we take a tour of the local caves and get some samples from the bats there?"

"Well, I guess that could be arranged."

"Good."

🌐✕🦇

"So, I guess we're of accordance that there was no leak from WIV?" said Dr. Chan.

"No. Their protocols are impressive. The equivalent of anything in the U.S. It must have spread from the bats to the local meat market and beyond."

"I concur. That's where we must concentrate our investigation."

So that's how our two doctors ended up donning Tyvek suits, breathing apparatus, etc., and exploring the bat caves west of Wuhan, China.

They were as astronauts marching through forested surroundings on an alien world, leading to the openings in the hills.

"I see many dead bats upon the floor," said Dr. Fernandez. "They appear to be juvenile."

"Yes," said Dr. Wang. "They are the most susceptible to disease. They are the first to die."

Dr. Chang pulled some samples from the dead bats. "I think we have what we need. Let's go. Dr. Wang, can you extract the genome from any virus there may be in these samples?"

"Sure. Let's head back toward the lab."

"How long?"

"Not long. Six hours; a day at most."

The next day in Dr. Chan's hotel room, once the results were in, the remainder of the plan went into effect. Dr. Fernandez spelled it out: "So one of the bats was infected with a coronavirus, and we have the decoded genome of it. Send the results of the genome extraction to the CDC. Explain how it matches exactly with the virus sample extracted from our fictional Seattle traveler. Furthermore, let them know about the shocking death rate among the sellers and shoppers in the Wuhan wet market. Immediate action must be taken to create anti-virus. Can you handle all that deception?"

"I must. I—must."

"Good man."

NINE

You Can't Go Home Again

D'Shaun's reply came back that same evening. *How about this Sunday? At noon?*

Before answering, Lola checked to make sure she had the address in her contacts. She did. *That sounds good. See you then.* She added a smiley face emoji, then changed her mind and backspaced over it. Lola felt a mixture of excitement and apprehension. *I wonder what sort of treatment to expect from Caitlin. Will Jadon be upset that I can't seem to remember times with him? Oh well, I find out in six days.* Lola went through her closet, trying to decide what to wear. "You know what? I think you need to buy your own clothes," she said to herself. Having made a few hundred shorting Acurmed stock, she was suddenly in the mood to go shopping.

Lola's mind wandered back to her life in Fordesboro, that now seemed to be so distant. How distant, literally, she had no idea. She could be millions of light years away, according to Dr. Fernandez. *You know what? I feel like taking a bit of a detour on the way to the Target store. O.K., maybe a large detour.*

That Tuesday, a day that began with a threat of rain, Lola grabbed her keys, set her previous life's address in Fordesboro into her cell phone, and stepped out the door. *I'm not even sure why, but I want to see the place.*

She drove according to her crowd-sourced traffic app, having told it to go the most scenic route, not necessarily the quickest. The view changed from urban to rural, getting hillier and more forested. The autumn coloration had lost a lot of its brightness. Evergreens filled the gaps between the shedding hardwoods. Leaves carpeted the ground. Lola didn't mind the overcast skies. Lola preferred less sunshine in her eyes when she drove. The orange leaves had seemed particularly brilliant this year. For Lola, of course, a second chance to see them had been quite a treat.

After about an hour and a half, the view became less bucolic as more and denser housing appeared. Traffic increased and progress slowed. A sign welcoming her to Fordesboro, a Tree City, USA, appeared on the right as she crested a small hill. Several stops and turns later, she pulled into the parking lot of the apartments she remembered as home, Vista Del Bosque.

There it is, number three sixteen, she thought as she glanced up from her position in the lot. She exited the car, slipped on a jacket, and took the stairs up to the third floor. Standing outside the door, memories flooded over her. Without thinking, she fished the keys out of her pants pocket, suddenly realized they would do her no good, and put them back. She began to turn and leave, then suddenly knocked on the door. No one answered.

Everyone's at work; silly. This was a waste.

A door further down the hall opened, and an older man came out. "If you're looking for Ned, he's probably gone to the Youth Sports Complex," he told Lola in passing.

"Oh yeah. Probably," she answered. *This is pointless, what would I have done if someone did answer the door. Oh, I used to live here, mind if I come in?*

"You can't go home again," Lola muttered to herself, and turned to leave.

"What's that?" asked the old man.

"Oh, I said; it may be goin' to rain."

"Well, I hope not. Have a good day."

"You too."

Shedding her jacket, Lola got back into her car. This time, she selected the quickest route to the store near her home; her new home.

After the emotional ups and downs of her detour, Lola's mood was buoyed by a couple hours of shopping for clothes, all the while wondering what meeting the Taylors was going to be like. *It's never as good or as bad as you think it will be,* she reminded herself.

Sunday arrived with a brilliant sunrise. After coffee and a croissant, Lola dressed in her newly purchased black jeans and burnt orange top. *Appropriate for a casual fall Sunday. At least I hope it is.* She watched the Sunday morning talk and news show until it was time to leave. Familiar trumpet notes heralded the announcement of the day's topics.

The day's trip would be much shorter than the day before, just across town. *Yep, I'm really doing this,* she thought as she pulled into what little traffic there was on a Sunday morning. She arrived at the modest but well maintained mid-twentieth century home much more quickly than anticipated. It was a few miles from the International Airport, just outside Charlotte's loop. It had a surprisingly large fenced lot. Parking streetside at the house on East Laurel Street, she sat for a bit and thought, *A third previous home. Two in as many days. One I remember, and two I don't. Well, I'm a little early, but no sense putting it off.*

She got out of the car, slipped on her dark jacket, and walked up to the front door, her heart beating faster with anticipation. She could hear a dog barking loudly in the back yard as she approached. The door swung open before she could ring the doorbell. A middle-aged African-American man answered the door. "Hey, Lola. Glad you're here. Jadon's been asking about you."

Hesitatingly, Lola spoke, "D'Shaun. Good to see you."

"Well come on in. Let me take your jacket."

"Sure. Thanks." Lola could not shake the odd feeling that she had seen him before. Not just in a picture at the apartment.

"Mommy, mommy!" came an excited cry from behind D'Shaun, Jadon rushed up to hug Lola.

"Jadon, how have you been doing?"

"I'm good. Missed you on Halloween. It was your turn to take me trick-or-treating."

"Oh, I'm sorry. You know, I've had problems with my memory lately."

"Oh yeah, daddy told me."

Lola took notice that there was no woman there to greet her. "So—Caitlin?"

"Oh yeah, you don't remember. It hasn't been going well between us, we separated a few days back. Poor Jadon, he now has two part-time moms. So make yourself at home. I'm grilling hamburgers out back, be ready in a few. Raffy won't stop barking until you go say hi to him."

Lola followed D'Shaun through the house and out the back door to the patio, where she was pounced on by a young white Labrador retriever. "Raffy," she said as she petted him, his tail keeping a beat.

"Yeah, you know, like Raphael," said Jadon. He seemed to realize she needed her memory refreshed.

"Oh, the cartoon turtle."

"That's it."

"Well, the burgers are done. Help me carry stuff in, Jadon," said D'Shaun.

"Smells good."

"I know you like charcoal grilling instead of gas."

They sat down around the kitchen table to a meal of hamburgers and potato chips. There were lots of appreciative sounds. "So, tell me Lola, what caused your amnesia?" asked D'Shaun.

"Uh, doctors say it's a dissociative amnesia state, probably due to some traumatic event. But it just came on suddenly for no apparent reason that I can come up with. Actually, while I was in the right seat on a flight. I'm obviously not on flight duty for now."

"Well, I hope your memory comes back soon. It must be disorienting."

You have no idea. "Yes, it is. Speaking of loss of memory, what is it you do again? I mean for a living."

"Wow, you really don't remember. I'm an IT manager. At SolAir. Cookies? Don't worry, there's no nuts in them."

"Thanks. Don't mind if I do. Yeah, there was a bit of an episode with peanut butter too, in the hospital. Forgot about my allergy."

"Oh, sorry."

"Do you remember how to play my favorite video game?" asked Jadon.

"Uh, sorry no. But maybe you could teach me?" Replied Lola.

Lola and Jadon spent the next couple of hours, her trying her best to get the hang of playing his game, and talking about fourth grade, and friends, and cartoons she had thought were long out of favor.

"Well, it's been fun, but I think I'd better get going now," she said as she set aside the video game controller after crashing a virtual car yet another time.

"Awww," said Jadon.

"I'll see you again soon. Right, D'Shaun?"

"Oh sure. Maybe next weekend, if you'd like."

After goodbye hugs from Jadon, She and D'Shaun walked together to the car.

"That was good," said Lola. "I have to ask. This may sound strange to you, but why did we split up? From what I can gather, it wasn't amicable."

"No. It wasn't. How can I put this? At the risk of upsetting you, you cheated on me. I assume at some point you'll remember anyway. I took it pretty hard."

"Oh, I'm sorry."

"Caitlin was kind of a whirlwind rebound affair, if you'll pardon the expression. Turns out we weren't exactly made for each other. She hasn't even visited Jadon since we separated. I'm glad you came back finally."

"I'm glad I did too," she said, and offered a hug, which D'Shaun accepted. "Well, bye for now."

"Bye—for now," he said as she rounded the car and got in. Pulling away, she felt better than she had in a week.

Back at her apartment, Lola checked text messages. There was one from Pascal. *Went through with investment. Paid dividends. Will reinvest. Repay me later.*

Lola smiled. It had been a good day.

TEN

Doctors but not Boarders

Doctors Chan and Fernandez toted their carry-ons through to security in the Wuhan International Airport. Their flight was right on time, and they had allowed for two hours prior to boarding.

Dr. Fernandez spoke, "I'm glad I was able to get my flight changed so we could fly back together. I could use some intelligent conversation."

"So, when do we meet this intelligent conversationalist?"

Both had a good laugh at that.

Dr. Fernandez stepped up to the security official's station and handed him his passport, turned to the photo page. The smartly uniformed official swiped it across a scanner, causing it to beep. He looked a bit perturbed, and did one more swipe across the scanner, resulting in a second beeping sound. For several seconds he stared at the machine's display.

This can't be good, thought Dr. Fernandez.

The official said something in Mandarin Chinese. Dr. Chan answered him, and then translated, looking concerned, "he said to stand to the side for a moment, and then asked me if I was travelling with you. He wants my passport now."

After scanning Dr. Chan's passport, he waved over what appeared to be two policemen, and spoke to them. One of them, who appeared to be in charge, spoke toward the two doctors.

"Oh my, they are the People's Police of the State Security Ministry. We are to go with them."

The two were led down a dim, dingy hallway and into a small room with a metal table and four folding chairs, trailing their carry-on bags. The room was harshly lit with fluorescent lighting and was uncomfortably cold. "Please, sit down," said the senior officer in English, as he motioned them to the side of the table across from the door. An airport employee followed them in, pulling along both of their bags that they thought had been checked through to the airplane's cargo hold. The lead policeman dismissed her, and unzipped a bag. He then glanced at Dr. Fernandez and asked, "is this your bag?"

After nodding in the affirmative, the policeman began to pull out the doctor's belongings.

"What is this all about?" asked Dr. Fernandez, clearly looking anxious.

"Quiet," was all the policeman said.

After going through all the items in the checked bags, they pulled out knifes and began to slash through the linings. Following that, they dumped all the carry-on items out onto the floor, and went through them one by one.

When their inspection appeared complete, the lead policeman spoke, "Now, tell us what was your purpose in your visit to the Wuhan Institute of Virology? To gain advantageous information for your United States government? Tell us now and it will go easier on you."

"Simply doing research on coronaviruses. We didn't really learn anything there, but we did get genomic information from an infected bat in a cave west of Wuhan. Bats that are sold in the wet market here."

"Genomic information?"

"Yes. DNA, the genetic code. Of the virus infecting the bat, that is."

"I see." Though it wasn't clear that he did. "Dr. Fernandez, perhaps you'd care to explain this," he said, holding up a photo of a passport. "We matched you to this passport using facial recognition software. Notice the name on it. Care to explain why you have two passports under different names?"

Dr. Fernandez looked briefly at the photo, then responded. "I had my name legally changed. Look at my old name. It was Morris Lester. Do you know what people use as a shortened form of Morris? It's Mo. Your English seems good enough to realize what that implies."

The look on the Policeman's face seemed to soften, eventually curling into a smile. His colleague followed suit.

"It was all fully legal. I believe Chinese citizens are allowed to change their names as well?" he added, glancing over at Dr. Chan.

"They can and do," concurred Dr. Chan.

"That passport was voided when a passport was issued for Doctor Tomas Fernandez. I have it sitting in a desk drawer at home with a hole punched through it. I see no hole in the picture."

The lead policeman said something in Chinese to the one who was clearly his subordinate. He said something back, apparently a simple acknowledgement of his order, and left the room.

"He sent him to do some further checking on the passport situation," said Dr. Chan to Dr. Fernandez.

"Yes. We wait now," said the remaining policeman."

After what seemed an hour, the man returned to the room, and spoke at length to his superior. Dr. Chan exhaled deeply and appeared relaxed.

"Well, it appears we still have some bugs to work out in our system of alerts. Your story does appear to check out. You may continue your journey back to San Francisco. I have relatives there, as it happens. Beautiful city. Cable cars and Lombard Street, yes? Good day to you." He walked out of the room and motioned for his subordinate to follow.

Dr. Chan seemed to want to say something more, but Dr. Fernandez cut him off. "I wouldn't say anything more about this until we're back in San Fran." He looked at his watch. He knew it was an anachronism, but Dr. Fernandez felt incompletely dressed without a watch. "If we really hustle, we may still make the flight."

"Do you want to get a new bag?" asked Dr. Chan.

"No. No time. I'm just jamming everything back in and hoping it holds. If it doesn't, no big deal. Everything I can't do without is in my backpack carry-on." Dr. Fernandez patted down the front of his shirt, feeling a thin booklet in his pocket. "Oh, thank goodness, I didn't remember getting my passport back. Let's go!" and he ran out towards the China Air luggage check-in for the second time, with Dr. Chan in hot pursuit.

Having rechecked their bags to San Francisco, the pair kept up their pace towards security. A look of recognition came over the employee's face and he waved them through, saying something to his co-workers in Mandarin. They were allowed to jog on through.

They hesitated for a minute while hearing their names announced over the PA system. Dr. Chan translated slightly before they heard the message repeated in English. "Air China passengers Chan and Fernandez, this is the final boarding call for flight zero, zero, three to San Francisco, at gate G12."

Once again picking up the pace, they arrived at the gate out of breath, shoving their boarding passes and passports at the gate attendant.

"Welcome aboard sirs, you just made it," she said, and picked up a phone and said something in Mandarin.

"What was that?" asked Dr. Fernandez.

"Only saying all passengers were now accounted for. Relax."

They took their assigned seats. Having arrived too late to get overhead bin storage, their carry-ons went under the seats in front.

"I can't wait until they start serving drinks," said Dr. Fernandez.

"Ditto."

♟∅✈

"Is it safe?" asked Dr. Chan, while they were waiting to see their luggage burst through the carousel curtain.

"Oh, you mean to talk about the Wuhan Institute of Virology?

"Yeah."

Dr. Fernandez glanced about, and seeing no one standing near said, "I think so. Call me paranoid, but I wasn't one hundred percent sure they wouldn't have surveillance on the plane."

"O.K., you're paranoid," said a smiling Dr. Chan.

"Oh, and I think it's time now to toss our checked luggage and get new bags."

"Sure. Hey I see mine now."

"Oh wait, we'll have to recheck the ones we have, go through security again, and get to our connecting flights. Never mind."

"Are you thinking the same thing I am though? If there wasn't much going on in the WIV around coronaviruses, why did our trip there draw so much attention?" asked Dr. Fernandez.

"Exactly. We seem to have stirred up a hornet's nest. I think especially in light of our 'evidence' of a jump to a human."

"Now we just need to prime the pump at the CDC. I'm thinking multiple jumps in additional cities."

"That's going to be a challenge."

"No worse than surviving a slip slide. I am so glad now that I did the name change completely legal. It was just my doc's creds that I paid for. I just can't believe my sliding double kept that name all his life here."

"You and me both. That was very stressful. I was picturing what Chinese jails might look like, and they weren't pretty pictures."

After handing over their checked luggage again, and going through security, they split up to catch their respective connecting flights.

"Well, have a nice rest of your trip. We'll talk again when we get home," said Dr. Fernandez.

"Bye."

ELEVEN

♀ ☎ 💬

Lola Wants to Know

Lola got up that Monday and spent the morning drinking lots of coffee and trying her best to remember what was going to happen in the stock markets soon. *I have less than five months to take advantage. Think!* But nothing came to mind. *Maybe when it gets closer to the slip slide date, I'll remember more?* She tried watching the show on the financial channel that covered stocks all day long, spitting out constant speculation mixed with business information. There was something that seemed to be in the back of her mind, nagging away, that needed to be addressed.

And there it was: *I had an affair? When? With whom?*

She didn't really feel it appropriate to bring up the subject with D'Shaun again. She wondered who might know, and would tell her as well. Lola only knew two people locally. She began with Pascal.

Surprisingly he answered the phone right away. "So, what's up Lola? I assume you got my message?"

"Yep. Thanks for lettin' me slide on paying you back, by the way. Makes for bigger gains."

"Oh, no prob, for an old schoolmate. And I'll only charge you twenty-five percent interest."

Lola wasn't sure if he was serious or not, but that seemed quite reasonable, especially given his line of work. "Listen, I have a very personal question to ask. It's concerning me, not you."

"Not sure how I can help, but let's see."

"How do I put this? You know I can't remember my past, right?"

"But you know the future."

"What I can remember of it, for almost the next four plus months. Anyway, it turns out D'Shaun and I divorced because I had an affair."

"Holy… Surely you don't think it was with me?"

"Well, no—and I may feel a bit insulted."

"Oh sorry. No, I just mean…"

"Relax, I know what you mean. But do you know anything about it?"

"Not about the affair, no. I always thought it was because of your gambling. You tended to lose—a lot. And not just to me. It even got worse after the divorce."

"Oh. O.K. So I guess it never came up."

"No."

"Well, thanks again. I'll let you go."

Lola then moved on to the only other person she knew that might have knowledge of her dalliance. She got Rita's voicemail and then it hit her that she probably still had a job to go to on a regular basis. "Oh, this is Lola upstairs. Just call me back when you can, O.K.? I have a question to ask you. Thanks. Bye."

Lola logged off of her trading account, and just spent the next few hours watching TV and relaxing. She had nearly dozed off watching a boring talk show when her phone ringtone snapped her back to attention. She saw that it was Rita calling her back.

"Hi Rita, thanks for calling me back so soon. I know you must be busy."

"I have a few minutes break from work. So what is it that you wanted to ask me?"

"Well, I'm trying to fill in a hole in my memory that I think is pretty important to know. This is rather personal, for me that is, I'll just blurt it out. I went to see D'Shaun and Jadon. Do you know anything about the affair I had that caused D'Shaun and I to get divorced?"

There was a noticeable pause at the other end.

"Uh, are you sure you want me to tell you? And right now?"

"I'm pretty sure. You know, the who, the when, et cetera."

"Well, this is pretty hard for me to go into, for reasons that will become clear."

More hesitation.

"I'm sorry, if it's touchy for you maybe…"

"No, no; you deserve to know, though it will be a—let's say awkward moment for the both of us. It was about two years ago. I started to say, 'do you remember,' but then… I found out that my boyfriend at the time, Rodney McLoren, with whom I thought things were going swimmingly steady, was cheating on me."

"O.K., sorry, but what's that got to do with my affair?"

"Really Lola? Do I have to spell it out for you?"

It was Lola's turn to be speechless for a while. Then, "oh, I'm so sorry, Rita. Yeah, this is awkward, to say the least."

"Yeah, he had a weakness for redheads. Oh, what am I saying. He had a weakness for any woman who could fog a mirror. It had gone on for a couple of months apparently. Then one day you were off duty, Rod was rarely working, D'Shaun came home early, and…"

"Yet, you're still friends with me?"

"Well, not for some time. But then I thought, he was a hard guy to resist, and he hadn't exactly put a ring on it yet. Forgive and forget. Friendships are more precious than love affairs, thought I. Then we had some good times together, you and I. Well, that's the whole sordid story."

Rita knew full well, it wasn't the whole story, but didn't see the point in adding chapter two. Certainly not yet.

"I know that wasn't easy. Thank you for telling me. Hey, you ready for that hike we talked about taking, next weekend?"

"You know I am. I'll call back later and we can plan it out."

"Sounds good. I'll let you get back to work now."

"Gee, thanks," said Rita sarcastically.

"Bye."

"Bye."

As Rita hung up, she thought, *I never thought I'd have to relive that episode of my life again.*

TWELVE

Outdoors Lola

Later that day, Lola suddenly remembered about an important earnings announcement coming up. She dashed back into the living room, and sat down at her desk to look up earnings announcement dates on her computer. "There it is," she said out loud to herself as she saw that database company Texas Information Management Resource, TIMR, was due to announce quarterly results tomorrow night. *That'll really pop after hours tomorrow, if I recall correctly. Then even more the next day.*

Having executed the buy order, Lola celebrated her future success with a glass of white wine. She watched the business news through the close of markets and the days wrap-up, then microwaved her dinner. Finishing up her chicken pot pie, she washed the few dishes she dirtied by hand, and placed them in the drying rack, just as there was a knock on the door.

Lola opened the door to see Rita standing there. "Come on in. By the way, you do know there is a doorbell, right?"

"Yeah, I just prefer knocking. I don't know why, but it seems less intrusive. I just stopped by to suggest we hike Pritchard Knob in the Pisgah on Sunday morning. Do you still have your hiking gear?"

"Oh, I think I saw some boots in the closet, a backpack on the top shelf, and a pair of trekking poles up there as well. Come take a look?"

Rita went through Lola's closet. "Looks like you still have everything. She pulled a fleece jacket, a watch cap, a pair of gloves, and a rain jacket out of the backpack. Finding a lightweight, waterproof pair of pants hanging up, she said, "looks like the pants you wore last time." Turning toward Lola, she said, "you have crew length socks to wear with the boots, right?"

"I think so."

"You dress in layers. An undershirt, lightweight outer shirt, those pants. And you start out with the fleece, cap, and gloves. It's chilly at altitude in the morning. Things come off and go in the backpack as you warm up. I think you're still set. We should leave at oh-dark-thirty Sunday morning, it's a two hour drive. Any later and a good part of the hike will be down a road just walking to the trailhead from where we have to park. I'll drive. Just meet me in the parking lot around sixish."

"O.K. See you then."

"Toodles," said Rita, waving as she left the apartment.

Lola wondered briefly whether or not to sit down and watch *Jeopardy!*, then thought, *Nah, I probably will remember so many answers. Or is it questions? What is: answers in the form of questions?*

🥾 🥾 ⛰

Sunday morning found Lola in an upbeat mood. Rita had offered to drive. Lola had not asked what car she drove, but figured it had to be the Jeep warming up, blowing condensation out the tailpipe at six a.m. on a crisp autumn Sunday morning. A wave from the driver's seat confirmed it. The parking lot was wet, from an overnight rainstorm, but stars could now be seen overhead.

As they got underway, Rita spoke, "So you can remember how to drive, do other day-to-day chores, use a computer and a cell phone, but you can't remember how to fly the jet airliners you've been piloting for so many years? And you don't remember me? That's curious."

"Yes, it is."

"Do doctors have an explanation for selective memory loss?"

"They say it's due to some trauma. But, ironically, I can't remember any trauma. Maybe it has to do with my job. It came on when I was in the right seat."

Lola wanted to get off the subject. "Rita, do you do any stock trading?"

"Only in my 401k funds. Why?"

"I have a few good tips for you if you do any retail trading. I can help you get started if you want. A couple of on-line brokers have just gone commission free, which is great news."

"So, you do this on the side? I didn't realize that."

"Yeah. On the side."

"Works out better for you than sports betting, I hope."

"Oh, much."

"Is there a minimum order?"

"Nope."

"Does sound interesting."

Lola managed to keep the conversation steered away from her "lost" memory until the stars could no longer be seen in the sky, and the already fading fall colors began to make themselves seen. They drove higher and higher, until Lola began to notice patches of white off to the side of the road. By the time they reached the trailhead parking area, the entire evergreen forest was dusted with a fresh white coat.

"Looks like a scene from a Christmas card," said Lola.

"Yes, comes early at over a mile high," agreed Rita.

"Must still be freezing out here. Glad I have all those layers. And gloves."

As they stood reading the trailhead sign, Rita said, "so two miles out to the peak. Take in the view, then head back. Rocky climb toward the end. Easy breezy. Looks like we're the first today," said Rita as she stared down the beginning of the unmarred white carpeted trail that led under some overhanging trees.

"So, should we be concerned about the bear warning sign?" asked Lola.

"Just a little. They're eating constantly this time of year, to get ready for winter. Make some noise every once in a while. They're just like us, they don't like surprises. Otherwise, they tend to leave you alone. If you see one, we'll wait until it leaves the area. O.K.?"

"O.K.," said Lola, not entirely convincingly.

"It's a bit muddy in spots where the snow has melted on the bare trail, but otherwise pretty good shape," said Rita as they leisurely headed out with her in the lead. Occasionally ice shook from trees overhead and fell on the two. Soon they emerged into an expansive meadow, the snow crystals on the far side beginning to sparkle in the rising sun.

At the other end of the meadow, a crossroads of sorts, beneath the base of the remaining climb to the peak of Pritchard's Knob. To the left promised a gentler climb, the right, steeper and rocky. Just the kind of challenge Rita loved. "Let's take the right trail. The left one is boring."

"O.K."

The right trail was a rocky ascent. The trail fell off sharply to their right side into thick forest. In some places stair steps were fashioned from rock, but most stretches were unevenly rock-strewn. As Lola slowly and carefully chose her path forward and up, she began to appreciate having the trekking poles for balance and to assist with climbing. Until now, she had questioned the need for them.

Rita stopped, turned to face Lola and asked, "doin' alright?"

"So far, so good."

Rita turned back around to restart her ascent. As she stepped up toward a large rock, a low guttural sound emerged from the woods to her right. Startled, she turned to look and her left foot missed its mark and stuck into a crevice in the rock.

"Bear!" shouted Lola. It was about twenty feet down into the forest, and standing on its hind legs.

Rita tried to remove her left foot, but seeing the black bear herself, miss-stepped with her right foot in a sudden nervous move, and it slid on a sloping icy rock. Her body fell over to her right, but her left foot did not go with her. A cracking sound was heard, followed by an ear-shattering scream.

The bear at this point lowered into an all-fours position, and was still and quiet, possibly unsettled by the scream. Then, possibly seeing Rita's fall as a threatening move toward it, began advancing slowly toward her and resuming its voicings.

Lola pushed back down on the fear that rose up inside. *I've got to help,* she thought. She remembered parts of a survival documentary she had seen. *Brown bear play dead, challenge a black bear. Make yourself look bigger.*

Lola spread out her arms wide, still holding on to the trekking poles. *Worst comes to worst, I poke at it with those.* Growling as loud and deeply as she could and waving her arms, her efforts seemed to pay off. Then the bear advanced a bit more. Again she growled and gestured. She wasn't sure if Rita's screams were helping or hurting, but she was certain they were going to come out regardless. *She must be in some serious pain.* The bear stopped and stared briefly, then turned and went back down the hill, with a few parting huffs.

Lola dropped the poles and shed her backpack. "Let me try to lift you vertical," she said to Rita, who by now was moaning loudly. Lola grabbed Rita under the arms and lifted, allowing Rita to place her right foot directly opposite her jammed left foot. Pulling it out of the crevice, she let out another scream, and fell on her backside. Rita's ankle was askew of her leg.

"Just lay down now, I need to splint your ankle," said Lola as she gently aligned it with her leg. "Now, try not to move."

Lola thought for a second about how best to make a splint. *Gather up a couple of sticks? Wait, the trekking poles.* She collapsed her trekking poles, then fished around in her backpack. "I know I brought some self-clinging sports wrap," she said out loud. She found the wrap, carefully laid the poles beside Rita's lower leg and ankle, then said, "I'm going to have to lift slightly to wrap you up. Ready?"

Rita nodded and tensed up. She let out another scream as Lola lifted and began to wind the wrap around the poles and Rita's leg, as tightly as she dared.

Having finished, Lola offered Rita a couple of aspirin and a drink of water, got her to sit up to take them, and removed her backpack. She used it as a pillow for Rita. Lola pulled out her cell phone. "Wow, we're in luck. I've got cell service."

"Nine-one-one, what is your emergency?"

Lola thought that sounded a bit sarcastic, as if to ask, "do you really have an emergency? Do you now?"

She described what had happened and where they were on the trail. "We had just started up the rocky climb that you go up if you take the right branch to Pritchard's Knob."

"O.K. Help is on the way. Try to keep the victim as comfortable as possible."

"Thanks. Yeah, I made a makeshift splint from poles and sports wrap. Seems to be in less pain now."

A half hour later Lola heard people calling her name.

"Up here, she shouted." As the rescuers came into view, she said, "you guys made good time. I'm so glad to see you."

They replaced Lola's makeshift splint with an inflatable version and loaded her onto a stretcher for the trip back out to the vehicle. "Good job on the splint."

"Thanks."

Rita spoke up, "where are my poles?"

Lola searched the wooded area where Rita had fallen and found her trekking poles. "Got 'em." She put her pack back on her back, Rita's on her front, collapsed Rita's poles and stuck them in Rita's pack, extended her own poles back to normal and followed behind the rescue procession.

She got the name of the hospital where they would be taking Rita. *Damn it, I missed the view Rita promised.* "Give me your keys. I'll drive your car to the emergency room."

"O.K. Here. I'll see you there. And—thank you so much. You literally saved my life."

𝕩 𝕩 ⛰

Later that afternoon, as Lola sat in the waiting room of UNC West Hospital's emergency center, a message appeared on her cell phone: *Two in a row. You go, girl!* ☺ *Pascal.*

THIRTEEN

Refresh My Memory

As time neared for the regular quarterly meeting of the Slip Sliders Club, the two doctors conversed on-line.

"I just read an interesting article in the *Seattle Sounder*," said Dr. Chan. "You may be interested to know that there was a report of an ill passenger arriving from China showing symptoms of an unknown corona virus. He had apparently shopped in a wet market in Wuhan, where they sell bat meat that was found to contain a virus. It was *apparently* discovered by a Dr. Wang at the Wuhan Institute of Virology."

"That is interesting. And it was reported by? said Dr. Fernandez, fully knowing the answer to his question.

"A Dr. Chan, who attended to the patient."

"Well done."

"The same Dr. Chan who reported it to the CDC?"

"The very same," said Dr. Chan, tongue firmly in cheek. "The CDC verified the report with Dr. Wang in China. And the circle is complete. They are working on a test for COVID-19. The Chinese are moving to create a test, also. They want to be able to quickly test meats in markets in and around Wuhan."

"Wheels are in motion. Good progress. We can report on it at the upcoming meeting."

Dr. Fernandez next called Lola to talk about a possible topic at the next meeting.

"Lola, until now only Dr. Chan and I knew about your backwards time shift from the other world. For a while I thought we should keep it that way, you know people will be wanting to take advantage of your foreknowledge. But then, you already have, haven't you? And so have Dr. Chan and I, albeit not for financial gain. So, I was wondering how you felt about letting the cat out of the bag, so to speak, and possibly passing on some tips for the members."

"Suits me. I have no problem with sharing the knowledge. And you're right, I've already helped myself and one other person. I can work on coming up with a list of stocks that I remember made big moves, and hey, I even remember what team won—uh, will win—the Super Bowl. A few months later and I probably wouldn't have."

"Sounds good. Our meeting is coming right up. You can share then with everyone at once."

"O.K. We've all been through enough, I think we deserve a little advantage. Oh, and I just had a thought. I remember you saying Todd remembered details about how to cause a reverse slide through use of hypnosis. Do you think that might help me remember some stock tips?"

"Hey, that's a good idea. I'll see if I can get a recommendation for a hypnotist in your area. It may not work out as well for you, since Todd had been prepped by a hypnotist as well, but I say it's worth a shot. And since you mentioned Todd, I want to let you know that he and Professor Gibbons have made great progress toward overcoming the biggest obstacle to the reversal process: the protective suit. We expect to be ready to go within a month or so. We're working to bring Dr. Gunter Feirstein at the particle accelerator in Raleigh into our confidence. It's called the Neuse Collider, because they study collisions of accelerated particles. Having some of your foreknowledge to use to convince him of our situations may certainly help."

"O.K. Yeah, I'll wait to hear from you about the hypnotist. Anything else?"

"No, I'll call you when I get a name. Bye."

"Bye now."

Within a few days, Dr. Fernandez got back to Lola with the name of a hypnotist, as promised. Roland Meinkes scheduled Lola for two days later.

"Glad you could see me so soon, Dr. Meinkes."

"Nope, not a doctor. I'm just a mister."

"Oh, sorry."

"So, Dr. Fernandez tells me you found yourself in a dissociative state, a sudden loss of memory."

"That's right. I have no memories prior to a few weeks ago when I seemed to magically appear in an airline cockpit."

"Interesting," said Roland, drawing out each syllable. "Is there any subject in particular you want me to question you about while you're in a state of hypnosis?"

"Yes. These glimpses of the future seem to keep popping into my head, but I can't seem to remember them all. Could you try to draw those out?"

"The future, you say? Interesting." Roland drew out the syllables even more.

"Uh-huh. Specifically, future visions related to business news. You know, new product announcements, earnings announcement surprises."

"A highly unusual request."

"I understand, but that's what I'm after."

"Unusual, but not actually the oddest request I've ever gotten. I'll give it my best. I must say, it's surprising that you're not interested in recovering your memory. Your actual past, that is."

A thought occurred to Lola. "There is one thing about my past that's been bugging me. I met this person recently, and he just seems so familiar, but I just can't seem to place him. His name is D'Shaun Taylor. Ask me about him?"

"O.K. Well, let's get started. I'll record the session, if you don't mind."

"Sure. Let's go."

"...and you'll feel refreshed," was the next thing Lola remembers hearing. "How do you feel?"

"Fine. Did we learn anything?"

"There were a few items of market interest you brought up that you actually claimed you 'remembered', but are actually yet to occur. I'll get you a transcript of those, plus you'll get a copy of the video. As to the question of D'Shaun, you did recall meeting him in college, your freshman year. He asked you on a date. To a concert."

"That's it! I turned him down. He never asked again. Not in my world."

"In your world?"

"Uh, never mind. Thank you," said Lola. She charged the session to her card, and left.

After Lola left, Roland got on the phone to Dr. Fernandez.

"You referred me quite the client. She 'remembered' things that *will* happen. The one thing that was a true—I guess—remembrance, she blurted out it happening in 'her world.'"

Dr. Fernandez seemed non-plussed.

"Did you get any stock tips from her?"

"She described some future market movements in some detail."

"Feel free to take advantage of them."

"You believe in that stuff?"

"From her, more than you imagine."

"Wouldn't that be insider trading?"

"That would be quite the gray area, wouldn't it? But who would believe your tout is an actual oracle who has foreknowledge? Who's the insider here? Anyway, I won't rat you out, and Lola doesn't care. Just don't make millions. And keep it to yourself. Who knows what other people would do for this info?"

"Now I'm curious to see if the first one happens. Well, bye."

"Bye."

Roland made another call after he got off the phone with Dr. Fernandez.

Hey, it's me. Roland. You're not going to believe who I just had as a client. Lola Sandborne."

He listened to the response and then said, "I've got some valuable info for you."

FOURTEEN

I'll Bring Salad and Regret

The phone rang. The caller was D'Shaun. Lola smiled and answered quickly.

"Hey, you're quite the hero," he said. "You stood up to that bear out there and likely saved Rita from serious injury or even death."

"Well, actually, I consider a broken ankle serious."

"You know what I mean, from a bear attack."

"O.K. But hero? I was saving myself."

"You're too modest. There was the running away option."

"Worst thing to do in that situation. In more ways than one. By the way, it sounds like you know Rita. Did she tell you about our encounter in the wild?"

"Well, yeah." Realizing she doesn't remember, D'Shaun added, "you and she were friends before you moved into her complex. We still talk occasionally. Also, there was an interview with the rescuers on the news. Anyway, I wanted to see if you would like to join us for Thanksgiving."

"Oh wow, that's next week, isn't it? Sure, that sounds great. What time?"

"Show up whenever, we'll eat around two."

"Great. See you around noon. Bye."

"Jadon's looking forward to it. Bye now."

What D'Shaun didn't say was that he was looking forward to it as well. Something, some quality that he couldn't quite put his finger on, seemed different about Lola now. *Good different.* Like things were at one time.

Then the phone rang later that day with a second invitation to Thanksgiving dinner.

Oh my God. It's mom. Cue the amnesia excuse yet again. "Hi mom."

"Lola, you haven't called in a bit," her mother said, lingering over her name.

"I'm sorry, mom. My life has taken an odd turn. I've actually lost most of my memory and I'm trying to get it back."

"I'm so sorry, dear. I do hope you remember me."

"That I do mom. At least I think I do. You still live in Knoxville, right?"

"Yes, same place for the last 36 years. Speaking of my place, you're going to be here Thanksgiving, right?"

This is going to be awkward. "Uhhh… Sorry mom, but I just accepted an invitation to go to D'Shaun's place for Thanksgiving."

There was silence on the line for moments. Then Lola's mother spoke, "Caitlin's O.K. with this?"

"They're separated mom. She doesn't even come over to see Jadon."

"Oh."

"I'll find a way to make it up to you."

"Don't you dare make plans for Christmas, other than here. O.K.?"

"O.K."

"Well, enjoy your Thanksgiving."

"You too mom. Love. Bye."

"Love. Bye."

After sunset that day, Lola went downstairs to check on how Rita was doing. Standing at the door, she reached for the buzzer, then drew her hand back, remembering what Rita had said about knocking instead. She balled her fist and rapped on the door.

"Who is it?" came a yelled response from inside, barely audible on Lola's side.

Lola was in a playful mood. She bellowed, "Housekeeping," in a high-pitched voice.

"Lola, that you?"

"You got me."

"Come on in, the door's unlocked."

Rita was half lying, half sitting on her couch, left leg on the cushions, right leg on the floor. "Grab a seat and watch *Wheel of Fortune* with me," she said, pointing to the kitchen table.

As Lola selected a chair and carried it to the living room, she said, "You always leave your door unlocked?"

"No, but that just saved me from having to hobble over there to unlock it."

"Oh, I see. So, you got back to work quickly."

"Yeah, I sit all day mostly anyway, in the doctor's office. Since it's my left ankle, I can drive. No clutch to work. Say, thanks again for what you did."

Praise had always made Lola feel uneasy, like she was an impostor who didn't deserve it. Changing the subject, Lola asked, "Think any more about dipping your toe in the turbulent waters of the markets?"

"Why not? It'll have to be my right toe, for the time being."

Lola chuckled. Suddenly she said, "Making small talk," in the direction of the television set.

Rita, looking incredulous, said, "you got that with three letters?"

"Must be a repeat?"

"Nope. First run."

Oops, blurted that out, didn't I? "Lucky guess."

After the bonus round, Lola asked, "ready to get started day trading?"

"O.K., my laptop is on my bed. Could you please get it for me?"

"Sure."

"Thanks."

Lola showed Rita how to sign up for a free brokerage account, then suggested a stock that she knew was going to pop come Monday. She showed Rita how to look up the ticker, figure out the number of shares she wanted to buy, and most importantly, create a maximum price she was willing to pay for those shares. "And then you select an order type of Good `Til Cancelled, or GTC. It's not actually permanent, but the system keeps it for many months."

"And it keeps looking constantly until the price dips below the maximum specified?"

"Exactly."

"For free?"

"Yep. It recently started being free. They get paid somehow, but I can't explain how."

Lola gave her a tip on what to buy before Friday close of business. "And remember, banker's hours, nine-thirty to four. You can place an order outside those hours, but the system won't try to fill it until nine-thirty."

"Got it. So, what makes you think this stock will go up next week?"

"They are going to—I have a good idea they are going to—announce much better than expected financial results after the closing bell Friday."

"They still use a bell?"

"The New York Stock Exchange still actually does, yes. They invite celebrities to ring it."

"Alright, we'll see what happens."

"So, I'm going to have Thanksgiving dinner with D'Shaun and Jadon."

"Really?" said Rita, drawing out the first syllable.

"Yeah, you know, I'm really looking forward to it. By the way, when he invited me, he mentioned that you two knew each other."

"Uh-huh." All that could be heard for nearly a minute were the chimes and clicks of the wheel against its pawl on the TV, comments from the host and guesses from contestants. Then: "It may be the pain pills talking, but there's something I want to tell you. You see, we know each other, uh, how should I put this, in the Biblical sense."

Rita paused a few moments, then went on, "we had met before, of course, since you and I were friends, but when you cheated on D'Shaun with Rodney…"

"You two both had a 'revenge' affair?"

"Yes." More silence. Then, "you don't seem all that shocked."

"Well, understand that since I couldn't remember either of you, this all seems as if it's happened to someone else. You know what I mean?"

"I guess I do. We were both ashamed afterward, and it's been kind of, you know, awkward between us since."

"I can see that."

"You know, it's been odd telling you all about your life, the parts you already knew, but even weirder telling you that for the first time."

"Ditto, for the weirdness factor."

"So... stick around for *Jeopardy!*?"

"Sure. Why not? What have you got to drink? I'll get it."

"Make mine a Chardonnay. Help yourself to whatever you want."

"Wine sounds good right about now."

Lola was happy to see that the *Jeopardy!* Episode was not one she had seen. After that, she asked Rita if there was anything else she could do for her. Of course, Rita said, "no," then she bid Rita good night and went back upstairs.

Well, this got complicated.

Later she turned on the nightly news to see if what had happened was still going to happen. Almost all of it did. *That's a shame.*

That weekend brought Lola a couple of congratulatory messages. First from Rita, in person, Saturday morning.

"Hey, that stock you talked about did announce what they called 'knockout' results. Should go up big Monday. You have some kind of inside info?"

"No, not really. It was just—let's call it—intuition. Did you make out on the buy?"

"Didn't actually pull the trigger on that this time. But, got any more intuitive thoughts?"

Lola did, of course, and enlightened Rita on what to do next.

Sunday evening brought with it this text message from Pascal: *Three-peat! Letting it ride. Happy Thanksgiving.*

FIFTEEN

Thankful for Second Chances

Lola arrived at the Laurel Street house around 12:15, grabbed a bag off the passenger seat, and walked up to the front door. Again, there was no need to knock. This time it was Jadon who opened the door. D'Shaun stood behind him.

"Jadon said he'd seen you drive up. Glad you decided to join us," he said.

Lola offered the bag to D'Shaun, freeing her arms up to hug Jadon. "I just put together a tossed garden salad. There's French and Italian dressings in there too. I went Euro themed."

"I'll put it in the fridge for now."

After Jadon and Lola finished hugging, D'Shaun had returned from the kitchen and offered the same welcome.

"Take your jacket?"

"Sure."

"Dinner will be ready a bit early, in about an hour. Something to drink? A Chardonnay?"

"Sounds good."

"Wanna try a different video game?" asked Jadon.

D'Shaun interrupted. "We're going to have football games on the TV, Jadon. Why don't you go out back and play with Raffy until dinner?"

"Oh, alright."

The back door was pulled shut. Raffy barked a greeting.

"He'll stay occupied for a few minutes getting Raffy to chase a ball. We used to watch the football games together, although I guess you don't remember. Still a Carolina fan?" asked D'Shaun.

"Uh, I still follow them," said Lola. *Not in the way you might think.*

"Rough couple of weeks for them, eh?"

"Yep."

"Caitlin has agreed to a divorce."

Lola didn't know quite what to say, and just muttered, "oh."

"I heard the B-17s are touring again and are going to be in Charlotte in two weeks, down at the Mecklenburg Hall. Would you like to see them?" asked D'Shaun.

Caught totally off guard by the invitation, Lola hesitated, then thought, *So,* that's *what he invited me on a date to go see back in school. This world's Lola must have accepted then. Now I can too.*

"You know what? I think I would."

D'Shaun smiled. They watched the football game, making occasional comments on it, until the back door reopened and Jadon appeared. "Raffy's done playin'. I'm hungry."

"You really interested in this game?" asked D'Shaun.

"Weeellll…"

"Me neither. Jadon, why don't you hook up your game console and take your mom to school on *It's Elementary?* Lola, you may be surprised by how much we either never learned in elementary school, or just flushed it out of our memory during summer break."

Jadon hooked up the console and showed Lola how the game worked. She felt like she was back in school, taking a test over repeatedly. Jadon of course getting most of the questions right immediately.

"Say, how many times have you already played this?" she asked him playfully.

"A lot, but I've never seen the same question twice."

"Oh," said Lola, dejectedly. The time passed quickly for the contestants, and D'Shaun announced, "it's ready. Let's eat! Ready for more wine?"

"Sure."

Any misgivings Lola had had about the day, melted away like the butter on the hot rolls. *I could get used to this,* she thought.

The conversation devolved to entreaties to pass something or other, or questions about whether more was wanted. It usually was.

"Your salad was great, fresh veggies," said D'Shaun.

"Glad you liked it. You really are quite the cook."

"Well, you know—I mean I guess you don't know, you were usually away somewhere exotic, like Kansas City. So, I was kind of a househusband."

That elicited a laugh from Lola, and D'Shaun joined in.

"Yeah, I miss those exotic locales, I think, maybe. Actually, no I don't think I would. I like it in Fordesboro—I mean Charlotte," said Lola.

After dinner, Lola said, "I'll help clean up."

"Thanks, but it's gonna take more than one dishwasher run."

"I've got time. Plenty of time."

After the dishwasher began chugging along on the first round of dish cleanup, Lola said, "Jadon, let's go out and play with Raffy, whaddya say?"

"Not a game?"

"I need something first that I won't lose at," she said with a wink.

D'Shaun watched the two taking turns throwing a ball across the back yard, with an occasional bounce on the patio giving a *ka-thwok* sound.

Could we actually make it work again? Jadon seems to have no doubts.

As daylight faded, Lola decided it was time to call it a day.

"Here's your jacket. I'll walk you out," said D'Shaun.

They walked out into the late fall afternoon air, which was surprisingly warm for Thanksgiving.

After opening the driver's door for Lola, D'Shaun said, "Pick you up at six show night? We'll go out to eat first?"

"Sounds good, see you then."

"Bye," said D'Shaun, and leaned in to give a peck on the cheek. Lola came back with a kiss on the lips, leaned back and said, "I think we had an audience," pointing to Jadon in the window.

D'Shaun laughed, turned and went back around the car to the sidewalk. He turned toward her car, watched and waved as Lola drove off.

Back at her apartment, Lola streamed a few song clips from the B-17s. Most of their music seemed to be fairly up-tempo rock and roll, but one song in particular caught her attention. It was one of their few slow-tempo, acoustic guitar based songs, written in a minor key: "Impostor Syndrome."

Sometimes I feel like I'm wearing a disguise,
made up of faded daydreams and outright lies.
I'm not at all who they think that they see.
Is that even someone I could ever be?

A soulful note-bending harmonica solo led up to the final chorus and its repeat.

Lola had found a framed picture of D'Shaun, Jadon, and her in a drawer of the desk. She took it out and posed it beside the school picture of Jadon that was already there. Staring intently at the family, she was lost deep in reflection, imagining an alternate reality of a family life, especially the family she saw in the photograph. She sighed and thought, w*ell,* is *it someone I can be? Why not?*

SIXTEEN

Start Spreadin' the News

Lola noticed that her current SolAir check was a lot lower. *Oh, that's the last of the sick pay.* Lola then found an FAA doctor who examined her and declared her eligible for short term disability. It would last six weeks, and then another determination would have to be made as to her status at SolAir.

The first Tuesday of every third month the Slip Sliders Club held their quarterly meeting. They got together online at six o'clock. The day and time had arrived. Darkness had already arrived in Charlotte, as it comes early in the waning days of autumn.

Lola wasn't as quick to get logged on this time. She had been thinking about Pascal's question of whether or not to take some winnings out, since the recent Sunday "victory," the fourth leg of their parlay. She finally decided, even though her sick pay at SolAir was drained, and disability had not yet started paying, her stock market gains were enough for now. As well as, a new stipend payment was coming her way soon. She texted: *Let it ride.* Then she just got connected to the meeting as six o'clock rolled around.

"I'm glad to see that you could attend, Roberta," said Dr. Fernandez. There's some news that you may be interested in, being the longest tenured in this world with a desire to return to your previous one. I appreciate you joining us, it being so late in your time zone."

Roberta Volina was an older woman, who specialized in software development in some of the older computer languages. "In my day, I was a programmer. Doubling the number of syllables in the title didn't make me any better at it," she once said. She resided in a suburb of Rome, Italy, so it was midnight for her. She spoke fluent Italian and English, *y un poquito de español.*

"Oh good, I see Professor Gibbons, of Southern Georgia University, is with us. He has news to share. And those of us who play the markets, financial and or sport betting, may get an early Christmas present from our new member Lola Sandborne. Nice to see you, Lola."

"Glad to be here," Lola said.

"Dr. Chan and I have been up to a certain adventure based on one of the peeks into the collective future here that was provided by Lola. It was a rather disturbing forecast, and we have been attempting to mitigate that. Dr. Chan will fill you in on our progress."

"Professor Gibbons, why don't you begin?"

"Thank you, Dr. Fernandez. We have managed to enlist the help of a physicist who works at the Neuse Collider near Raleigh. He is Dr. Gunter Feirstein. With his assistance, using the knowledge gained from Todd Longrain through the use of hypnosis, we have come up with a protective suit for use in the reversal process. It was quite a challenge to get it lightweight enough to not be too cumbersome to use. The doctor has been able to test that it withstands the synchrotron radiation produced inside the collider tunnel, under the guise of validating a protective suit for maintenance workers. A mannequin has stood in for a worker, or a reverse slider candidate. Of course, it could actually be used as such, as protection against inadvertent exposure.

Some of you may have heard of the Russian physicist that that actually happened to. He stuck his head inside a particle accelerator, not realizing it was on. They don't actually make a lot of noise. The left side of his head was paralyzed, and he lost hearing in his left ear. However, the part of his brain through which a hole was drilled was apparently one he could still live without, and he suffered no other long term effects. He even went on to complete his PHD.

It's not likely that episode could be repeated, given that modern accelerator beams are completely sealed in and very narrow. Only the sympathetic synchrotron radiation between the beam and the tunnel wall is needed for our purposes." The professor paused to let the attendees process his story.

"So, this suit is basically a Faraday Cage version of a beekeeper's suit. A special addition that a worker would not have, is a valve through which gases can be vented from an inside pouch. Releasing a small quantity of a mix of certain noble gases into the tunnel was given as part of the process under hypnosis by Todd. That will create quite a light show, like the aurora borealis, only much brighter."

Jon Fredricson, the real estate broker, spoke up, "Professor, why do we have to be sneaky about this? Can't we just get all the scientists involved? Seems like just the kind of real-world application, feel good story they would want."

"Believe me, we've tried. Even though the theory is pretty much accepted by all or most of academia, it's still career suicide to claim an actual occurrence," said Professor Gibbons.

"It's like acknowledging UFOs could be piloted by non-terrestrial beings, even though most scientists agree that in an unfathomably large universe, we can't be the only populated planet. Try getting your experiment funded after claiming a disc landed in your backyard and little gray men got out. Or women. Or whatever," interjected Dr. Chan.

"Exactly. Now we've only tested for protective integrity, we won't know if the mind swap will actually work until one of you tries it," said the Professor.

"I have a theory that in the near-worlds we came from, there exists an equivalent of our little support group. Furthermore, I think they also have quarterly meetings on the same exact schedule, and that your counterpart joined the group as well. Now, Roberta, given the time and date you gave us when you slid over here, I've worked out the time differential between this world and your counterpart's. I place the next meeting of your counterpart at December 19, three o'clock, our date-time. I think it best that the reversal happen then, so your fellow slip sliders can help to reorient you," explained Dr. Fernandez. "Of course, we will be on this end to assist your counterpart."

"How long do you expect the process to take?" asked Roberta.

"It's nearly instantaneous, once you release the gases. You briefly see the light show, maybe a second, then *poof*, you're somewhere else. At least your mind is. Didn't I explain in the special meeting?"

I didn't attend."

"Oh, right."

"So, Roberta, do you think you can arrange to meet us at the Neuse collider the afternoon of December 19? You'll be the first to go back." continued Dr. Fernandez.

"Sure. I'll be there."

"O.K. Now, if you will Dr. Chan, bring the rest up to date on our, not so little, subterfuge?"

"Sure. Thank you, Dr. Fernandez."

Dr. Chan proceeded to spill out the tale of their somewhat harrowing trip to, and "escape" from, Wuhan, China. He brought them up to date on their attempt to speed up reaction to the oncoming pandemic, to try to lessen its spread and impact.

"So, you're telling us that you suspect a pandemic is coming because Lola talked about it. Which means her world is future shifted?" asked Jon.

"Exactly," replied Dr. Fernandez. "I had some qualms about releasing that information at first, but not anymore. Her world of origin was about five months into the future, and it was a very-near world, meaning much or most of what happened in it, will happen here. Which I think, is a good segue to our next subject. Lola, care to offer up some tips?"

Lola cleared her throat, then began, "In my previous world, I almost exclusively supported myself by trading of financial instruments. That is, stocks, stock options, currency exchanges. I was fairly good at it, less some glaring misses. I remember most of the great successes, and *all* of the big misses. I have documented those that I could remember, dates and details of what happened, that affected prices. Check your e-mails, I sent it to all of you just before the meeting. Additionally, I know that due to the coming pandemic and associated lockdowns, the S&P 500 will be heading downward early February of next year. It will lose thirty five percent of its value by early March."

"Keep in mind our attempts to ameliorate the pandemic intensity, and what lesser impact a lesser pandemic may have," interjected Dr. Fernandez.

"If anyone needs help with setting up a brokerage account, or with trading fundamentals, let me know. These tips can be taken advantage of to help you financially," added Lola.

"As well, they can be helpful in building up our club funds," added Dr. Fernandez. "Though we'll steer clear of the sports gambling. Strictly legitimate, above-board stocks."

"Isn't that considered insider trading?" asked Todd.

"Ummm… I mulled that over myself. A reason I held back the knowledge of her future awareness. As I told Lola's hypnotist—gray area. I mean, who's the insider? I now kind of consider the gains as reparation for our situation," said the doctor.

Lola continued, "also, I have some football future news for you. Carolina loses their last eight games of the season. Those of you inclined to bet, you have four games left. I have a parlay going myself. If anyone wants, I can put them in touch with my local—for want of a better word—bookie. Oh, and no huge scoop here, New England wins the Super Bowl. Another month and I probably would have forgotten who even played. Already forgot the loser."

"Thanks, Lola. Now you would be the second one to have your slip slide reversed. I calculated it needs to be done January third, around four o'clock, to put you in a June meeting."

"Uh, doctor, about that. I have become adjusted to the life I'm leading here. I see no reason to go back, I've adjusted well, financially, socially, and possibly romantically, so…"

"Oh. That's surprising. Well, in that case, does anyone have anything to add?"

There were several "thanks" extended to Lola, then silence.

"Alright then. Don't forget, our next meeting is March the third. Roberta, let me know when you arrive in Raleigh, the professor and I will meet you. Goodnight, all."

"*Ciao*," said Roberta, mixed in with a chorus of other parting statements.

The next day, Pascal called. "Lola, the parlay is getting too big to be handled by anyone I know locally. I've got to lay it off somewhere outside of Charlotte."

"O.K. Why do I even need to know?"

"Just so's you're aware. If it takes me a long time to find someone, I may miss next game."

"Fine. That still leaves three more."

"Glad you understand. Do you want to know just how big it is now?"

"No. Surprise me come New Year's."

SEVENTEEN

♀ ? ♀

Inquiring Rita Wants to Know

The next day, after Rita got home from work, she called Lola. "Hey, why don't you come on down for a drink? Or drinks?"

"Why not? See you soon."

Lola knocked and heard a faint, "come in," from inside.

"O.K. I just made some money off the second tip you gave me," Rita said before Lola even had a chance to take a seat. "So, sit down and tell me, how do you know this stuff? Is something illegal going on here?"

"Nice to see you too. So where's that drink?"

"You know where everything is now—again. Right?"

"Yep, same for you?"

"Uh-huh. Now spill."

"Well, first of all, there's no law against using what you see in the future, as far as I know."

"You see the future?" said Rita, incredulously.

"To be clear, not so much see it, as having lived it, at least the next four months of it."

"Now you're scaring me."

"Sorry, didn't mean to. May as well lay it all out for you, then you can make up your mind whether to believe it or not. I won't go into the physics of what's happened, let's just say I haven't lost my memory, I've actually lost my body. It's in another, alternate world to this one. God knows where it is from here."

"Ohh-ee-ooh. Getting scarier. Did I mention that the doctor I work for is a psychiatrist?"

"Don't get the butterfly net just yet. Hear me out."

"Ohhhh-kay."

"Apparently minds can swap complete memories across great distances. Instantly. No one knows what triggers it. But it's scary."

"Scarin' me and I still remember who *I* am. So you're saying the pilot mind is in a body somewhere else, and your mind is in the pilot's body?"

"Very good. But we're both Lola Sandborne. I, however, was just working from home, trading stocks, et cetera. Now, as it turns out this has happened to others. They called themselves slip sliders, and have formed a club, a sort of support group. There are a couple of doctors and a college professor in it. You care to talk to either of them about our situations?"

"I'll give it some thought. But I'm not sure exactly what could help me wrap my head around this. Maybe another drink?" she said as she raised an empty wine glass. "And to the top this time."

"Maybe a few more correct 'predictions' will do the trick."

"Maybe."

"Isn't it time for *Jeopardy!*?"

"Yeah," said Rita, grabbing the remote. The familiar tune issued from the TV as the host appeared on the screen with his trademark permanent smile.

That contestant looks familiar, thought Lola.

By the time double jeopardy started, Rita had stopped asking, "how did you...?" She checked the program metadata to make sure that it was not a rerun. It was a first run show.

"O.K., you can stop showing off now," she said. "You were never *that* good at trivia. Either your story is true, or you're a witch. I prefer to believe your story. That must have been harrowing."

"It was, at first. I seem to have adapted pretty well now though, if I must say so myself."

"I agree."

"Our club just had a meeting. It was announced that we're ready to try a process that can reverse the switcheroo."

"So, when do you go? When do I get the old Lola back? I kinda got used to this one, actually."

"I decided I like it here. I'm doing pretty well financially, after starting from a hole. And you're a good friend. But mostly, I think I'm falling for D'Shaun. I really like him, and I like Jadon."

"He's a cute kid. And—well—you know."

"Yeah, I know. I can't believe you never told the alternate me."

"Well, I can't believe I told *this* you."

"You do realize this means I will never 'remember' our past together, right?"

"Yeah, I do. So, four months from now, your superpower goes away?"

"Right. Back to poring over financial reports, and doing the opposite of what the so-called financial wizard celebrity on the business channel says, to make my money."

Rita laughed at that. "The oooolllld-fashioned way, as the commercial went."

"I eeeaaaarn it," Lola said. They both had a good laugh.

"By the way, D'Shaun and I have a date next week, at the B-17s' show."

"Oooohhh, sounds like it's getting serious—again."

There was a brief pause in the conversation, then Lola resumed with, "so, another month and we try to find a bear-free hike?"

"You bet."

"Funny you should mention that."

Lola clued Rita in on the parlay with Pascal that was halfway through, and asked if she wanted in on it.

"Why not? I'll take a piece of that action. Four more games, right? Geez, if I double my money each time... Is that possible?"

"Maybe. Depends on the book odds, of course."

"Correct me if I'm wrong, but if I let it ride each time, and it doubles each time, that's a sixteen-fold increase?"

"Your math is fine."

Rita stared at the ceiling, apparently deep in thought, then said, "holy cow. That means if you started at game one of eight..."

"I did."

"Two hundred and fifty-six times your original bet?"

"Your math is again, correct. Although, I'm not expecting quite that much. Maybe close. Maybe not. But, mathematically speaking, a shitload."

Rita laughed again, then proposed a toast: "to the next four months."

EIGHTEEN

🕵 🔲 🤝

Todd's Mission: Accepted

December seventh, Todd awoke to the ringing of a telephone in a Motel 6 in Amarillo, Texas. Shaking off the grogginess of sleep, he realized that the ringing phone was a wake-up call, and picked up and set back down the receiver. He sat up and looked around. Work boots sat on the floor at the foot of the bed. Winter coveralls with the company name WindWalkers and their propellor logo emblazoned on them hung in the small closet. A couple pair of jeans and plaid shirts also hung there. In the drawers he found some long sleeve undershirts, underwear, and thick crew length socks. There was also a fleece lined jeans jacket He dressed in the civvies: jeans and a red plaid shirt.

Todd took the smartphone off the night stand and held it to his face. It unlocked for him. He spent quite some time scrolling through old e-mails, looking for correspondence relating to the slip slide reversal process. There was extensive correspondence from a name that he did not recognize. The person seemed to be intimately involved with implementing the process. Todd decided to visit him first.

Todd found keys in the night stand next to the bed, marked with the Ford name. The motel room key card was also in the night stand. He grabbed it as well, pulled the coat on, and headed out to find the vehicle. It was parked right outside the door. An unlocking click on the key fob elicited a verifying response from lights and horn. He started the truck, let it warm up for half a minute, then took off for the airport. He needed to book a flight. May as well do it at the airport, maybe he could catch one at the last minute.

He parked the truck in the long-term lot, and placed the parking ticket that he had received on the dashboard. He put the keys in the center console and locked it using the driver's door keypad. He headed to the SolAir check in desk.

Todd got on standby for a flight early in the afternoon and went through security. He ordered a coffee at one of the chain cafes near the gate for his standby flight, and sat down at an empty table. He pulled out his smart phone, and looked at it to pop it into readiness. He read news articles until his name was called and he checked in at the desk. He would board with the last group, but he was on his way to his destination soon. Having rarely ventured out of the western U.S., he wondered what it looked and felt like. During the flight, he pulled a cord out of his shirt pocket and recharged the phone.

Nearly six hours later, Todd found out. He was struck first by the greenery of the landscape, as they approached the airport. After landing and deplaning, he headed immediately to a car rental agency, with no baggage to collect. The next contrast was the amount of moisture he felt in the air, even in winter. He hired a car, a small, economical Kia, and he was on his way to his first destination.

His first stop was a store that sold him an air pistol that looked just like the real thing. He also purchased a package of large zip ties. The clerk didn't ask any questions. It wasn't the kind of place where questions were asked.

His next stop was a modest house on the outskirts of town. It appeared that there was no one home. He pulled up and parked curbside, went to the door and knocked just in case. No answer. He went back to his warm car and waited. He passed the time listening to talk radio. It featured two sports commentators jousting back and forth. He found them humorous.

About six p.m., the person he was looking for pulled into the house's driveway in his dark four-door SUV. He got out and walked slowly to the front door, inserted the key, turned it and opened the door. Todd had sneaked up behind him, pushed him inside and pointed his air gun at him as he spun around.

"Hello, Dr. Feirstein."

"Todd? What the…"

"I need to see your computer, all backups, and all printed material on the slip slide reverse process. Let's go."

The previous day, in another world that was nearly one hundred years more advanced than Dr. Feirstein's, their Todd, the one later accosting him, was being prepared to undertake a mission of great consequence. The head of the recently formed National Applied Physics Agency, or NAPA, was giving Alternate Todd his final briefing.

"As you certainly know, some few years back a group of physicists here took it upon themselves to put their knowledge to use to reverse the quantum entanglement switch between you and your doppelganger in an older world. Well, they should not have."

"Yes sir, that's been made perfectly clear to me. A third switch will swap us again. When I am back in the other world, I proceed with operation 'One Way Street.'"

It had been made perfectly clear to him through the use of drug enhanced programming, to permanently implant the thought processes required to proceed. It had to be permanent, as any drug-related only effects would stay with the body.

"Good. Are you familiar with a very old science fiction series, *Star Trek?*"

"Yes, sir. We studied it in Classic American Fiction class in college."

"Did they mention something called the 'Prime Directive?'"

"Yes, the crew of the *Enterprise* were not allowed to interfere in any culture that they encountered. They must not influence it, only study it."

"Exactly. Well I'm afraid that's what those physicists did here. They sent back advanced knowledge of how to reverse the mind swap, back to a less advanced world, albeit not that less advanced. You follow me?"

"I do, sir." It was a final rehash of the same thing that had been drilled into Todd for weeks now.

"You are now fully aware of the scope and seriousness of your mission? You are ready to accept what must be done?"

"I am aware, and do accept," Todd said, in a flat monotone.

"Good. Because if they were allowed to proceed with that ability, our best AI has determined that they would advance to where they could initiate the swaps, not just reverse them. Who knows beyond that? And it—we have concluded that they're not ready to handle that ethically. It's not an easy decision to make, but such expertise must not be allowed to remain in their grasp. It is a matter of utmost importance that we right the wrong that has been done."

"I understand."

"Now get some rest. We initiate tomorrow at ten a.m. Target Todd should be sound asleep in his domicile at that time. When you wake up in his body, the plan must be put in motion."

"Very good, sir."

At that, Todd was dismissed. He rose, turned and left. As per his instructions, he left to get some rest. He did feel tired. The drugs and the programming had left him weary. They had overcome his natural instincts and turned him into a soon to be planted agent, ready and willing to do their bidding.

As it turned out, Alternate Todd had turned up at Dr. Feirstein's doorstep in Cary, NC, on the seventy-eighth anniversary of the surprise attack on Pearl Harbor. Neither the physicist nor the U.S. Navy had been prepared for such an occurrence.

"What's going on here, Todd? Why are you doing this?"

"Into the kitchen. Go."

"Alright, *Gunter*, now sit down in that chair. Todd nodded toward the kitchen table's captain's chair. Take these two zip ties and tie *your* legs to the chair legs."

The physicist did as he was told.

"Good. Now loosely zip these ties around the arms and your wrists."

"O.K. Now with your teeth, pull both tight. I'll know if they're tight or not."

Having seen that his instructions were followed, Todd headed toward the Dr. Feirstein's office. He came back out with the physicist's laptop computer and sat at the kitchen table with it, across from Gunter. "Password, please."

Gunter hesitated.

"I *said, password please!*" Todd waved the gun at him, hoping that it was real enough to fool him. It was.

Todd spent the next half hour working away at the laptop. Then, satisfied with his work, he turned to Gunter. "Where are the printed documents?"

"Why would I print them?"

"Wrong answer," said Todd, and went around the table to backhand the physicist across his mouth. "Where are the printed documents?"

Dr. Feirstein proceeded to tell Todd about his hidden safe, including the combination.

Todd came back out with several manuals on how to reverse the slip slider process. Seeing that the PHD Gunter had a wood-burning fireplace in his house, he tore out some pages as kindling and threw them in. He lit those and followed up with the manuals, one at a time, as the fire grew. Dr. Feirstein said nothing. His countenance spoke for him.

"Any more copies, hard or electronic?" said Todd.

"No."

Todd watched him closely, looking for any sort of tell.

"Who else has any?"

Gunter didn't answer immediately. Then, "No one." He choked a bit on the *no*. That earned Gunter a punch in the gut.

"Again, who else has any," said Todd, more forcefully.

After getting his breath back, the physicist answered, "Professor Gibbons is all. But you knew that, right?"

"No. But you thinking I did, confirms it."

A lightbulb moment occurred to Dr. Feirstein. "Oh, you're Todd from the other world. You were sent back here to stop this world from using the technology. Why? What changed?"

"Leadership changed. They decided that our scientists overstepped their bounds in allowing that capability to come back with the other Todd. It's a wrong that needs righting. By any means necessary."

That last statement sent a chill down Gunter's spine.

"O.K. We're going for a hike, you and I," said Todd, flicking open a pocket knife that he had also purchased recently. He cut the zip ties with his left hand while still menacingly pointing the gun with his right. He held it off to the side to help hide the fact that it wasn't really a firearm. Not that the physicist would have been able to tell. "Now, go change into outdoorsy type clothes."

Gunter headed to his bedroom with Todd following closely behind. The physicist changed into a pair of blue jeans and a long sleeve pullover shirt. He covered that with a zip-up fleece. Warm socks and boots went on next, then a watch cap. He grabbed a heavy coat to fight off the cold night air.

"We're going on a hike? At night?"

"Yep. Let's go. You're driving. Your car."

Gunter led the way to his car as Todd closed the front door behind them. Gunter popped into the driver's seat. Todd slid into the back seat directly behind him. "We're going to Lover's Leap Falls. Obey all traffic laws. And remember, I'll have my gun on you and will be watching the route on my maps app."

Dr. Feirstein placed his own smartphone in a dashboard cradle and pulled up directions. "It's over an hour away," he said.

"I've got plenty of time."

Gunter latched his seatbelt, started the car and pulled out of the driveway.

A tense, quiet hour later, the physicist turned off the paved road onto a gravel one. At a gravel parking lot just large enough for four vehicles, he pulled up to a weathered sign that read:

Lover's Leap Falls Brink Trailhead
.8 mi. to brink of the falls

At that time of night in such a remote location, theirs was the only vehicle in the lot.

Todd bailed out in a hurry, and stood near the driver's side door. Gunter got out slowly. His mind was racing, trying to come up with a way to disarm and subdue Todd. He had never been in so much as a schoolyard scuffle before. *Just try to keep calm and think straight. Wait for the right opportunity.* He pulled on his overcoat.

Todd handed him a headlamp. Yet another recent purchase. "Here. You'll need to see to lead the way." He slipped it over his watch cap, turned it on and proceeded down the path. Two peculiar thoughts intruded: that he didn't lock the car, and that the trail would be spooky to take alone at night.

It was a fairly easy trek for the first quarter of a mile, then it began to climb, with some rocky outcrops to scramble over and the occasional stairsteps formed by dirt-filled log frames. Gunter began to breathe heavily, and was actually becoming hot under his coat.

"I need to take this coat off."

"No, you don't. Keep moving."

At least let me unbutton it."

"Alright. But keep moving."

After another quarter of a mile of gaining altitude, the out of shape physicist was actually perspiring. Then the trail flattened out a bit. A crescent moon sporadically peeked out from behind clouds. It didn't provide much ambient light. It was hard to tell in the dark just how high they were relative to where they started. Gunter thought he could hear the sound of rushing water as his labored breathing returned to normal. The trail made a sharp right turn. Soon it paralleled a creek, the source of the sound.

"Falls Creek," said Todd.

The surrounding environs began to appear more and more rocky. Some fairly large boulders could be seen in the beam of Gunter's headlamp. The rushing sound became louder and louder. The slight moon was obscured by a cloud. They came to a sign positioned to the right of the trail beside an eight-foot high, six-foot wide boulder. The boulder reminded the physicist of a giant gumdrop in the headlamp beam. The sign read:

Caution: Sheer Dropoff Ahead

"You really don't have to do this."

"I'm afraid I must. Just a few more steps."

At that, the physicist took one step past the sign, simultaneously switching off the headlamp, plunging them into total darkness. He hunched over and dashed around to the other side of the boulder. He could feel spray coming off the brink of the falls.

"You're just delaying it," Todd shouted, as he switched the gun to his left hand. He put his right hand on the boulder, to guide him as he began to circumnavigate it. Todd cursed himself for not bringing his own light.

Todd heard a rustle, then felt a shove on his right shoulder, sending him toppling sideways, then another that sent him falling backwards, into the roaring waters of the creek. He lost his grip on the gun and it fell into the water. At this time of the year the water was not particularly deep, but it left the rocky bottom extremely slick. Todd attempted to stand up, but only succeeded in losing his balance, and he slid ever closer to the brink of the falls. He was close enough that the increased force of the water took his initial momentum and sped him over the edge, with Todd clawing frantically at the slippery creek bottom. His screams lasted only about two seconds, the time it took to fall seventy feet to where Falls Creek resumed its more closely horizontal journey.

Dr. Feirstein sat on a small boulder and began to sob as the constant fear of the past couple of hours drained out of him. Even knowing that it was totally justified as self-defense, he felt pangs of remorse. Eventually gathering his composure, he turned on his headlamp and searched for the gun. He found it near the creek bank, trapped under a log. Laying down on the creek bank, he reached down and fished it out of the water. He shook it dry, then stuck it in his inside coat pocket. He pulled out his phone and checked for coverage. There was none. With a deep sigh, he began to retrace his steps back down the trail.

At the point where it began to descend, he found that it is actually more difficult descending than ascending, though it was less tiring. He got to his car in half an hour, and headed back home. He knew he would never be the same again.

NINETEEN

Aftermath

As soon as Dr. Feirstein had cell service, he pulled over to the side of the road and placed a call. "Dr. Feirstein? It's getting late."

"I know it is, but thank God you answered. You should be sitting down. I've got an unbelievable story to tell you. I need some help, and I thought of the Slip Sliders Club, and you in particular. I just don't know where else to turn."

Dr. Feirstein went on to tell Dr. Fernandez the entire story, including Todd's fall to his death.

"That is incredible. Now, are you sure that Todd died?"

"Fairly certain. I heard him scream for nearly two seconds, then a thump, then nothing. That works out to at least a seven-story free fall." There was silence for a while, as Gunter hoped the physician would be forthcoming with advice. Then he decided some prompting was in order. "What should I do? Call the police?"

More silence, then, "probably not. You'd have to come up with a story more believable than: he was sent from another world to destroy your work and kill you. Let's just let it be an unfortunate hiking accident."

"O.K.," said Gunter. The thought suddenly occurred to him that he was going to have to cover up a crime in which he was the intended victim.

"Now, you'll need to get Todd's car back to the trailhead lot so it will be found in the morning. You'll need some help with that, to get back home afterwards. It wouldn't be a good idea to deal with strangers who pick up a rider in a remote area late at night."

More silence as Tomas was thinking. Then, "there's no way I can get there in time to help. I think you're going to have to try to enlist Lola's help."

"She's three hours drive away, in Charlotte."

"I know. Still, that's your nearest option. You need to get her to meet you at the trailhead parking lot, and take you back home."

"O.K.," came the wavering response.

"Hang in there, it's going to be alright."

Dr. Feirstein wasn't so sure.

"Now, a couple of things. When you drive Todd's car back, wear gloves. Don't adjust anything, if you can avoid it. Else, make sure you set everything back the way it was when he drove."

Dr. Feirstein was a little unnerved by Dr. Fernandez's advice. "Have you done this sort of thing before?"

"No, but I read a lot of suspense fiction. The *Decker: MP* series, specifically. Those two slipups came out in the last two books I read. Never did I think that would become useful knowledge."

"Yeah. Wild."

"Well, that's all I have for now. You should call Lola as soon as you can. Time is of the essence now."

"Right. Thank you, doctor. I'm sorry to have to get you involved."

"Well, Alternate Todd kind of already involved us all, didn't he? Goodnight and good luck. Call me tomorrow morning when everything's done. Don't leave a voicemail. I'll turn up my ringer so I'll be woken up."

"Thanks again. Bye."

"Wait. One little detail. Do you have Todd's car key?"

"Oh crap. I've got to go back. I was hoping to not have to deal with his body. Bye."

⚠ 🏛 ⚠

Lola's favorite Thursday night TV lineup was nearing its end when her phone rang. She was inclined to let it go to voicemail, but when she looked and recognized the name, she decided to answer. For the second time that night, Gunter related his predicament.

"I'm sorry to drag you into this, but after talking with Tomas, Dr. Fernandez, we concluded you were the nearest possibility for help. Even though I'm not actually a slip slider, I was hoping for some help from the club."

"You've been of tremendous service to the club. So yeah, I guess I'll help. It's a three- hour drive from here, so I need to get started."

"Thank you. Remember, meet me at the Lover's Leap Falls trailhead. Your map app should get you there, I think. I had no cell service at the lot. Make sure to download a map of the area before you go. Know how to do that?"

"I'll figure it out. Bye."

"O.K. Right now I've got to head back there and retrieve Todd's car key. Luckily Dr. Fernandez thought of that before I got back home and realized I didn't have it."

Gunter pulled back on to the highway, headed in the opposite direction, back toward the falls. As he approached it, his level of apprehension increased proportionally. He recalled seeing a sign for a separate trail that went to the bottom of the falls. He hoped it wasn't long. It seemed to take longer to return than it did to get to where he had pulled off the road. In actuality it was quicker, as he drove faster.

As he pulled into the parking lot, he was at least grateful it was still empty. Remembering the advice that Dr. Fernandez had given him, he opened the glove box. Dr. Feirstein was the rare sort who actually used the glove box for—gloves.

"Well, I won't have to wonder anymore how spooky it would be out here, at night, by myself," he said to himself. "Looking for a dead body, to boot."

Dr. Feirstein stepped out of his SUV, mounted and clicked on his headlamp. He found the sign that read:

Lover's Leap Falls Base Trailhead
.4 mi. to base of the falls

Half as far, and probably flat. Good, he thought, and set off down the trail. His imagination began to take over and he fought to overcome the fear that seeped in. He imagined all manner of nocturnal predators. *I wonder if this is sasquatch territory?* But nothing stirred. "I have to do this, I have no choice," was his mantra. It helped a bit that the skies seemed to be clearing, but not much, as very little of the moon was lit.

Finally, after fifteen minutes that seemed to go on and on to him, he heard the modulating splashes of water. The sound grew in intensity with each step, until he could feel its spray. Gunter swung the beam around the base of the falls several times, but saw no body. What he had dreaded finding, he now feared the not finding even more. *Could he have survived? No. Floated away downstream?* One more sweep with his headlamp and something caught his eye. It was a shoe sticking out behind a wide boulder. The physicist started walking across the slippery rocks, his arms outstretched for balance. At one point, no rocks stuck above water level, and he resorted to wading. He was knee deep at one point. The water was freezing cold. Finally he was on the other side of the boulder.

There was Todd's body, splayed out grotesquely. *Let's get this over with,* he thought. He avoided gazing directly at Todd's face, its unseeing eyes gazing skyward. Dr. Feirstein winced and bent down to the highly objectionable task. Sticking his hand into Todd's wet jeans pocket, he was rewarded with the feel of a key fob. He breathed a sigh of relief. He pulled it out, put it in his own pocket, and immediately began the return trip to his car.

He hustled it back to his car, partly out of a strong desire to leave, partly to try to generate some heat. His legs felt frozen. He was soon back in his car, engine running, heater on full. He pulled out of the lot and restarted his journey back home.

An hour later, he drove down his street. His headlight beams bounced off of Todd's older model Kia. He came to a stop beside it. Gunter pulled the key fob out of his pocket with his still gloved hand. A click on the open padlock symbol brought a chirp and a flicker from the car. Another relief. He pulled his own car into his driveway. Just one more trip to make before the night was over. He took off his gloves, went inside and made some coffee, and poured it into an insulated tumbler. He changed into dry pants. If he left to go back now, he would hopefully only have to wait half an hour at most for

Lola to arrive. Maybe less. The last thing he wanted to do was keep her waiting.

He put his gloves back on and went to the Kia. He got in and familiarized himself with the controls. Gunter searched the glove box and found a rental agreement. Ye Olde Jalopies was the company name. It was a low price. He started the car, checked for adequate fuel, and pulled away. Gunter had not adjusted the seat or mirrors. He and Todd were of similar stature. He was headed to the Lover's Leap Falls Trailhead parking lot for the third time in what was now two days.

Along the way he sipped on his coffee. He had time to think on the way. The one thought that kept recurring was that that the Todd that they had known, who returned from another world, would now be stuck there forever. His slip slide partner on this end no longer existed.

Dr. Feirstein pulled into the trailhead lot for one last time. He parked, turned off the engine, and waited. His wait only lasted twenty minutes when another vehicle pulled next to his. As its door opened, the dome light came on. A woman stepped out.

"Lola?" said Dr. Feirstein.

"Yes. Dr. Feirstein, I presume?"

"Yes. I'm sorry we have to meet face to face under these circumstances. Thank you so much for coming. Well I guess we can..." A sudden realization hit Dr. Feirstein. "Oh no. I have to go back to the body again. The car keys. They have to go back in his pocket."

"I'd say so. Is it far?"

"No. I should only be half an hour there and back. God, I hate to have to see his body again. Even though I know it's not him, he looks like the same Todd who was working with us. Just lying there in that stream. Never doing anything again. There's no avoiding it. I wish I'd thought to bring dry pants with me this time," he said as he headed down the dark trail once more. "Uh, do you happen to have a flashlight?"

Lola nodded in the affirmative and grabbed a small handheld flashlight from the driver's door pocket. Dr. Feirstein thanked her one more time and disappeared into the darkened woods.

Less than a half an hour later, Lola saw a light growing brighter along the trail. It bounced from side to side. Soon, Dr. Feirstein appeared behind it, and switched it off. "Here you go," he said as he handed her flashlight back. "It's done. Let me grab my coffee and lets get out of here." He took his coffee tumbler, pushed the door lock plunger down and shut the door. He got into Lola's car, and with a crunch of gravel, he felt he was finally leaving the site for good. The memories would never leave, he thought.

Back at his house, Lola asked Gunter what he had done with the gun. He went back into his study and retrieved it. "I'd better take that with me," she said. "I'll get rid of it in Charlotte."

Dr. Feirstein thought of thanking her again, but that seemed to be getting tiresome. "O.K. So I understand you've decided to stay in this world?"

"Yep. I'm not going to do the reversal. I kind of like the way things are going here. Past five hours excepted, of course. Look, as much as I would like to stay and talk, I need to find a motel to get a few hours rest before I head back. I'm beat."

"Why don't you crash here? The couch opens up into a bed. I can let you have mine. I'll change the sheets."

"No, don't do that. But I will take you up on that couch."

"Perfect. I'll get you covers and a pillow. Would you like something to drink?"

"Got any white wine?"

"Chardonnay alright?"

"Perfect."

Dr. Feirstein poured her wine and himself a scotch and water. Both began to relax a bit.

"I've been thinking a lot about the other Todd," said Gunter. "He's stuck now in another world. It's far ahead technically of what he's used to. I sure hope he can get by, because his way back is gone now."

"Yeah. That is sad. But don't think it's your fault, in any way, shape or form. You only did what you had to do."

"Sure. I know that's true. But still—you know?"

"I know."

"Hey, on a lighter note, you're a double hero now. You saved Rita, now you've saved me. Here's to you," he said as he raised his glass.

"How'd you know…"

"Oh, I pay attention to the news. The story, and the interview with the paramedics, was on the Raleigh station. Kind of as a public service precautionary tale about bear safety while hiking."

"Wow. Well, I'm ready to hit the sack if you'll kindly provide my bedding," she said as she put her glass down.

"Sure."

Dr. Feirstein got Lola's bed ready, then went in his own bedroom and closed the door. He wasn't sure when he would be able to get to sleep.

Four hours later, Lola snapped awake. She got up slowly and looked down the hallway to Dr. Feirstein's bedroom. The door was still closed. She thought about waiting until he got up, but instead wrote him a note, left it on the kitchen table, grabbed the gun and left the house. She wasn't sure, but she thought it was just a pellet gun.

Dr. Feirstein got up and called in to work. He was staying home. He walked bleary-eyed into the kitchen and found the note. He called Dr. Fernandez. Tomas answered. Gunter told him he thought everything was under control now. Some hiker would probably find the body today. It should be chalked up as an unfortunate hiking accident.

"So, how are you doing?" Tomas asked.

"Better than I thought I would be, this morning. Lola was a lifesaver."

"Well, I thought of one more reason you should have no remorse."

"What's that?"

"If he had been successful with—you—you know, he almost certainly would have headed to Georgia and Professor Gibbons next."

"Yeah, I guess he would have. Thanks doctor."

"Don't mention it. You probably could use more rest. I'll let you go. Bye."

"Bye."

He was right. Dr. Feirstein got some more rest.

The evening news carried the story of a hiker's body found at the base of Lover's Leap Falls. It was the body of a male of possible Native American descent, Todd Longrain. The case was being treated as a hiking accident, an apparent fall from the trail at the brink. Documents found in his car indicate that he flew here from Amarillo, Texas. He was apparently a wind turbine technician who worked for the WindWalkers company. No word yet on where he was staying locally, or if he had intended to do more than explore the Carolina wilds while in the area. Anyone with knowledge of this person was requested to call local police or 911.

TWENTY

Impostor Lola, Pioneer Roberta

Over the next few days both Lola and Dr. Fernandez called Dr. Feirstein at various times to check up on how he was doing. As expected, the trauma slowly began to wear off. Lola was the first to stop calling him, and after a week, so did Tomas. Relief began to push out fear and anxiety. A kind of unwritten, unspoken taboo settled around the entire incident. Life for the three resumed somewhat normally, though never completely for Dr. Feirstein.

One day later, Lola had introduced Rita and Pascal, and she was now in on a four-game parlay. Four days after Lola's revelation to Rita, game loss five was added to Lola's, Rita's, and Pascal's total. Lola still did not want to know just how much it was up to, but Pascal seemed to be becoming anxious for her to take out some of her winnings.

"No, let it ride," she had said. "I assume you already took out for yourself what I owed?"

"Oh, quite some time ago. You know this is in cash, right? A lot of cash."

"Get a safe deposit box. Buy a safe. Take it out of my account."

"I have a safe—But… Well, O.K."

One week and one day post revelation, it was time for her date with D'Shaun. He showed up at the promised six o'clock, then waited for a few minutes before going up to her apartment. When Lola heard the doorbell ring, she at least knew it wasn't Rita. She opened the door and greeted him with a smile.

"Hi!"

"Lola, you look sharp."

"Why, thank you."

"So, is Italian food O.K.? There's this place near the Meck…"

"Sure," she jumped in. "Is that what the cool kids call Mecklenburg Hall now; the Meck?"

"Probably not now."

"I'm ready, let's go," she said as she grabbed a purse, stepped out of the doorway, and locked up.

The ride downtown was a bit awkward, but she managed to break the ice by asking about Jadon.

"Oh, you probably don't remember, but Sarah from down the street is watching him tonight. Jadon likes her. We don't have a curfew."

"I'm sorry to have to have my life explained to me, but how did we meet? At college?"

"We did meet, at college, and went out a couple of times. But then went our separate ways after graduation. Then, coincidentally we met again at SolAir. Got married a year later."

"Wow, that was a coincidence."

"Yeah, small world."

Small, but there are so many of them.

After a satisfying dinner of lasagna, they went to the concert venue.

D'shaun held up their tickets for validation, and they passed through to the lobby.

"Wow, this place is beautiful inside. Look at the woodwork, and the art," said Lola.

"Yes, it's quite old. We're second row, left side, seats 15 and 16. Like a drink before it gets started?"

"No, I'm good, thanks."

Unlike their early days, the band rushed on to the stage only five after as colored lights circled about them, rolling off the fake fog that spilled over the edge of the stage. The crowd roared in anticipation of hearing all their favorites at a rate of decibels. Midway through the show, the B-17s settled down for an acoustical set, featuring of course, "Impostor Syndrome."

I am, aren't I? The other me made this relationship, and I just come along and think I can fix it up and then own it?

The show ended after the obligatory, "good night," followed by the waiting of a patient audience for the requisite three-song encore. "We hope you enjoyed the show," said the lead singer as they again marched to stage right. The conditioned audience knew it was over for certain then, and headed to the exits with a great murmur and rustle.

They entered into the night air, which had cooled considerably. Lola pulled on her jacket for the walk to the parking spot he had found two blocks down. As they settled into the car, D'Shaun said, "great show."

"Yeah, I loved it."

"You seemed a bit distracted later on."

"Oh, just; you know some of the lyrics really make you think."

"Sure. Will you join us for Christmas? At least for dinner?"

"O.K. Same deal as for Thanksgiving?"

"Sure. Great."

They arrived in the apartment parking lot.

"Walk you to your door?"

"Thanks."

Lola opened her door, turned to face D'Shaun, planning to ask him inside, but instead said, "thanks for a wonderful night. Let's end it here, for now, O.K.?"

"O.K."

Lola leaned in for a kiss and a hug. After they separated, she said, "see you Christmas."

"I had a really good time. Goodnight." He turned and headed for the stairs.

One week after Lola and D'Shaun's concert date, at the directed time, Roberta Volina was standing outside the Neuse Collider building with Professor Gibbons, Dr. Gunter Feirstein, and Dr. Fernandez.

After introductions, Roberta said, "that's a pretty small building. There's a particle accelerator in there?"

"That's just the entrance and lobby," said Dr. Feirstein. "The actual collider is underground. Follow me, please," he said as he led the group through the entrance, swiped his badge for each person, and they then boarded an elevator. Once they were all in, he punched a button labeled "*h*." Seeing the quizzical look on her face, he said, "Stands for Planck's constant. Inside joke."

The elevator stopped and opened up into a control room. They stepped out, Roberta did so hesitantly.

"Don't worry, no radiation here. In fact, the accelerator is not running now. I'll start it up when you get set," said Doctor Feirstein. "Let me show you the inside."

He opened a hatch door and stepped into a tunnel, which seem to curve slightly in toward them as it went off in each direction. It seemed to Roberta a hopelessly complex tangle of piping and wiring. It was quite sterile looking.

After a brief introduction to how it worked, he led her back into the control room.

"We have the place to ourselves, right now. As far as my associates are concerned, I'm strictly running a test on the suit. They didn't show much interest," said Dr. Feirstein.

"Roberta, you're absolutely sure you want to go through with this? You know you're the first to even try it," asked Dr. Fernandez.

"I'm ready," she simply said. "Let's do it."

She was helped into the protective suit by the professor and the doctor, as Dr. Feirstein spooled up the particle accelerator. "The suit has a radiation detector built in. When it detects sufficient flow, a red LED light will light up in your visor. That's when you can turn the valve and let the gas out, then hopefully, goodbye. And, well—hello. Now remember, wait until you're in the tunnel, facing correctly, the hatch is closed, the light comes on, to turn the valve and release the gas," said professor Gibbons.

"Got it."

"And you know which way to face?" asked the professor.

"Go through the hatch and face down the tunnel to my left."

"Good."

Once the suit was secure, Dr. Feirstein stood in front of the suited Roberta Volina, so she could see him through the faceplate, and gave her a thumbs up. "We're ready. Are you?"

"*Sí*. Yes. I'm ready to go home," came the muffled reply.

Roberta walked toward the open hatch she was shown, walked through it, and turned left.

The professor shut the door. Dr. Feirstein, at the control console, spooled up the accelerator. They could watch what happened next on video monitors.

The light in Roberta's suit hood visor turned red. She turned the valve, releasing he noble gas mixture. Suddenly blazing multicolor lights sparkled and danced inside the tunnel. The professor and the doctors noticed her turning to her right, then her left. She started to fumble with the front of the suit, where it closed up.

"Shut it down!" yelled the professor. "She's trying to take the suit off!"

"Then fellows, I think it worked," said Dr. Fernandez.

"We're shut down now," said Dr. Feirstein.

Dr. Fernandez opened the hatch and walked over to Roberta. He took her by the arm and led her through the open hatch into the control room. He and the professor helped her finish getting out of the suit. There was a confused look on her face, and she looked shaken. "Where am I?" she mumbled.

"In a particle accelerator. In its control room now. In your old world. Did we get you out of a meeting?" asked Dr. Fernandez.

"Yeah… How? What?"

"Good. Welcome back, Roberta. We reversed your slip slide, right in that particle accelerator tunnel. You are the first to be brought back by us. I'm Dr. Fernandez, by the way. We need to talk about your current situation in this world, and whether or not you want to go back to Italy."

"*Sí. Molto*. Very much. My Italy, yes?"

"Yes."

"I'm going home."

"Then maybe you'd like to share your experience with our version of the club that I assume you were embraced by in the other world. Professor Gibbons here is a member," he said as he pointed the professor's way.

"I think I would."

"Good, by the way, you're in the United States right now. Raleigh, North Carolina. We'll get you a place to stay here while we arrange to get you back to Italy," said Dr. Fernandez.

"*Molto bene.* very good."

An e-mail went out to the SSC members: *The very first slip slide reversal initiated by us occurred today. It was successful. The original Roberta is going to resume her life in Italy.*

TWENTY-ONE

🦉 🔔 🌲

Joy to the World—and That Other One

Lola and Rita celebrated Christmas Eve together down at Rita's apartment.

"You know, I'm having second thoughts about these gambling winnings. It's going to be in cash, right? So how do I spend it without getting in some kind of trouble—attracting the wrong kind of attention?" said Rita.

"I'm wondering that myself. Pascal may be able to help you there, help us both. Not really up on this sort of thing, but I'm guessing we're probably O.K. if we don't run afoul of the IRS. Declare it as gambling winnings on your tax return. You won it less than six hundred dollars at a time, so no ten ninety-nine. Or you made it selling stuff at the flea market, other income. Just a couple of thoughts. And just spend it very little at a time. If it really is bothering you, just tell Pascal to only give you as much as you think you can handle," said Lola. "The stock gains shouldn't be a problem, tax returns get a little more complicated, but there's good tax software out there to make it easier."

"Yeah, maybe just my original bet back. I'd sleep better. I'll give it some thought. Maybe put the rest in an envelope and send it to a charity: an anonymous donation."

"Anyway…" Lola raised her wine glass toward Rita and said, "merry Christmas and a happy New Year."

"Merry Christmas. May it be a great new year."

🦉 🔔 🌲

Christmas day Lola stopped by Rita's on her way out to spend the afternoon at the house on East Laurel Street.

"Merry Christmas. It's Santa Claus. Sorry I'm late, my sleigh broke down, and I had to call the Sled Club."

"It's O.K. Come on in. Your voice sounds a little high pitched, Santa."

"Heater quit on the sled, too. And get a fireplace, will ya?"

Both had a good laugh.

"Here you go," Lola said, and handed Rita what was obviously a wrapped bottle of wine, likely white, likely Chardonnay, likely way overpriced. She had D'Shaun's and Jadon's gift in a separate bag with her.

"And here you go," said Rita, and handed Lola just as obvious a gift. "Headed over to the Taylor's house?"

"Yep. What are you up to?"

"Oh, headed over to mom and dad's later."

"Oh crap; mom. Sorry, I need to call her and wish her a merry Christmas. I'll see you later, Rita."

"Bye. Enjoy your visit."

"You too."

"Hardly," muttered Rita.

Lola tossed the bag on the passenger seat of her car, started it to get it warmed up, then ran back up to her apartment to get out of the cold air while she called her mother. She shed her coat, and rang her mother. After the usual greetings and well wishes, Lola told her that she would try her best to come see her soon.

"It doesn't have to be a holiday, you know," said her mother. "Especially since neither of us are working right now."

"I know, I know. Love you mom."

"Love you too."

"Bye."

"Bye."

Lola put her heavy coat back on and hurried out to the car. *I hope it's still there. Probably not the brightest idea.* It was, blowing out clouds of steam as the now warm engine heated the moisture in the exhaust. The bag of gifts still sat on the passenger seat.

Phew. She no longer needed turn by turn directions to get to the house. Traffic was light on Christmas Day, she got there much more quickly than her previous two trips. The house was tastefully rimmed in blinking lights. An arguably less tasteful vinyl snowman inflatable stood sentinel as Lola strode up the sidewalk, with her bag of gifts.

Again the door flew open as she neared it, and Jadon rushed to hug her.

"Mommy!"

"Jadon. Merry Christmas."

He grabbed her by the hand and led her into the house. D'Shaun was standing in the kitchen, tending to the cooking; or at least watching it.

Lola pulled out a small wrapped package and handed it to Jadon. "Here you go. Betcha can't tell what it is."

"Video game!"

"I was wrong," said Lola, with a false tenor of resignation in her voice. Striding over to D'Shaun, while Jadon tore at the wrapping, she said, "and for you, drinkie-poos." She pulled out another object which was clearly a wrapped bottle of probably wine, probably Chardonnay. "And, it's not even a regift from Rita."

Lola thought she caught a hint of a wince from D'Shaun at the mention. He stepped away from his chef duties and accepted it. "Thank you."

"It's not that I'm above that. It could have been awkward if she came up for a drink later, and I didn't give her a drink from her own gift bottle."

He laughed, with a just-there hint of nervousness.

They hugged and gave each other a brief kiss on the cheek. Jadon was already sitting in front of the TV, thumbs frantically pounding at the buttons on the game controller.

"I see you got him a game that he doesn't mind playing by himself."

"Yeah. Not that I don't mind joining him."

D'Shaun poured a glass of wine and offered it to Lola. She took it and sat at the dining room table. He poured himself a glass and joined her.

"So, Jadon has been telling me you seem a lot happier lately. He wants to know if you are going to stay here and be his only mom again?"

I kind of hope that happens too, she thought.

"Frankly, I've been wondering that myself, lately."

"So—all water under the bridge?"

"Under the bridge, downstream, and out to sea, as far as I'm concerned." After a noticeable silence, D'Shaun continued, "I'm sorry. I'm making you uncomfortable, and it's Christmas." Quickly changing the subject, "what the hell has happened to Carolina? Seven losses in a row, and most not even close?"

"Yeah, who would have thought they'd fall apart like that?"

"I know."

"So, will you at least be joining us for New Year's Eve? Well, mostly me. Jadon isn't staying up 'til midnight."

"Oh, I'm sorry. I already promised Rita that she and I would spend it watching fireworks. She doesn't have a date, either."

Lola thought he may have pulled away a bit at the second mention of Rita.

"O.K. I won't push you anymore. Let's just enjoy Christmas dinner together."

"Sure, thanks."

And they all did seem to enjoy it, Jadon even asked for extra green bean casserole. They told Lola stories about the good times they had had together, as if she wasn't even there, which of course—she wasn't. Raffy eagerly lapped up offerings from his bowl.

Then, after helping clear the table and get a dishwasher run going, Lola's internal "time to go" alarm went off. "This has been a really good Christmas. I think I should probably go."

"You don't have to."

"I know, but…"

D'Shaun led her to the door, opened it and followed her out, after a goodbye hug from Jadon, who went back to master his new video game. At the car, they hugged and kissed, and exchanged, "see you later."

Lola dialed up Rita while still on the road, something she was normally loathe to do. Surprisingly, she answered.

"Rita, in the unlikely event D'Shaun calls you, you and I are doing New Year's Eve together. O.K.?"

"Sure. Like you said, unlikely."

"Yeah. But if you don't have anything else to do, maybe we could get together and watch the fireworks somewhere."

"Why not?"

"O.K. Bye."

"Bye."

When Lola got back to her apartment, the next call was to Dr. Fernandez. This time it went to voicemail.

"Dr. Fernando. First of all, Merry Christmas. But also, please give me a call when you can. I'd like to discuss something with you. Again, Merry Christmas. Bye."

TWENTY-TWO

⚠ 🚹 ⛓

Rita's Turn

The Friday after Christmas, Rita came home from work, and discovered her apartment door was unlocked. There didn't seem to be signs of forced entry, and thinking she must have forgotten to lock it before heading to work that day, opened it and entered. She came face to face with an unwelcome guest in the form of her old boyfriend: Rodney McLoren. More than that, there was an extremely unwelcome nine millimeter handgun pointed at her.

"Hello, Rita. Happy to see me?"

"Bloody hell, Rodney. Have you gone bat-shit crazy?"

"Like a fox."

"What do you want from me?"

"All I want from you is to get me in to talk to Lola."

"Why don't you just go talk to her?"

"I wasn't sure I remembered her apartment. And you are going to be leverage."

"What do you want to talk to her about?"

"About—the future. I need more of it."

"Huh?"

"I know she knows what's going to happen, with stocks, with football games, with diseases. I want that. I need that. I started with next to nothin'. I've got a little more than nothin' now. I need to know more, much more."

"Then you know everything she knows—and I know. Her knowledge only goes five months out. Well, only about three months now."

"Bullshit. I want to know the rest. Let's go," as he waved his gun toward the door. "What apartment are we going to?"

"Two-oh-six."

"That better be right," he said as they climbed the stairs to the second floor balcony.

They approached the door to apartment 206. Rita started to knock, and hesitated, then pushed the doorbell button.

Inside, Lola had settled in to watch local news. She yelled out, "Who is it?"

"It's Rita."

Rita? She never uses the doorbell. What's goin' on here?

Lola creeped up to the door and looked through the peephole. A man she did not know was behind Rita. "Who's that with you?"

"Bitch. You know who it is. Now open the goddamn door!" Rodney said, as he stepped sideways to Rita's right and pointed the gun at her head.

"No, she doesn't. She's lost her memory. I thought you knew?"

"Oh, yeah. Well never mind. Open this door now, or…"

Just as Rodney uttered the *or,* Rita swung her right arm in an upward arc, followed by a left cross to his solar plexus. The gun flew up and clattered to the balcony floor. Immediately, she bent her right knee and brought that foot up and to the rear, into his crotch. He collapsed to his knees with a loud moan.

Lola, having seen the pretty much one-sided fight through the peephole, opened the door and stepped out as Rita shoved Rodney prone and put her right knee on his back. She pulled his right arm behind his back and held it there. He howled.

"Got any zip ties?" said Rita.

"I don't think so."

"Go down to my apartment. Kitchen island, bottom left drawer. Bring the pack of the large white ones." As Lola took off, Rita added, "hurry!"

It seemed to take forever for Lola to reappear with the ties, Rodney groaning and complaining the whole time, but in fact it took less than two minutes.

"Pull his left arm back."

Lola did and Rita quickly secured his wrists, as if she did that every day.

"How…"

Spinning around on her knee, which elicited more groans, Rita took another zip tie and bound his ankles. With him now fully trussed, she explained, "FBI academy. I didn't make the grade, obviously, but I did pick up some defensive moves. And how to neutralize a dangerous suspect. Never actually thought I'd get the 'chance' to use it, though."

"Still, that was quite a chance you took, with a gun to your head."

"Not as much as you think. I noticed the idiot had the safety on. Probably isn't even loaded. He was never the one to think things through. What did we ever see in him?"

"Uhh…"

"Oh, yeah," Rita said with a knowing smile.

"Why did he want to come here?"

"He thought you had more tips he could use, and he was going to force them out of you."

"And then?"

"Like I said, he wasn't one to think things through."

"How did he even know about my future knowledge?"

"No idea. Check his pockets?"

Lola rummaged through his pants pockets. She pulled out his wallet, opened it and pulled out a business card.

Roland Meinkes

Hypnotist

"That's the hypnotist I went to. Rodney, you knew Meinkes?"

Rodney just moaned, a bit lower this time, and managed to say, "just let me go and I promise to never bother you again."

"The two of them must be in cahoots. Roland pries out valuable information, and Rodney takes advantage of it. What are the odds?" said Lola. "Well; you've certainly paid me in full for the hiking episode; and then some. Your ankle O.K.?"

"Surprisingly. We're even Steven now?"

"Oh yeah. I'll call nine-one-one."

"Please? Roland put me up to it," said Rodney.

"Wait. What do we tell them?" said Lola.

"Whaddya mean?"

"How will it sound: he wanted me to tell him more about the future?"

"Sure. Who will believe him? Maybe they'll go easy on a crazy guy, huh Rodney?"

Silence.

"Let me call. You go down and meet them in the parking lot so they can see you're not armed. You can explain exactly what happened, from when I rang the doorbell to the takedown. They can get a little overzealous before they have the situation they aren't sure of under *their* control," said Rita. "Tell them the gun is a few feet away, on the balcony."

Hours later, after Rodney was in custody, and the police had their stories, the two sat tighter in Rita's apartment, beginning to decompress.

"I've got something to tell you," said Lola, breaking a long silence.

"Well, that's never a good lead-in."

"I've changed my mind. Well, I've changed my mind about not changing my mind, back to the other world's Lola."

"Oh? I was really getting to like the new Lola."

"I was getting to like you, also. And obviously D'Shaun, and Jadon. And the money coming in."

"So, where's the bad?"

"Unfortunately, I have a conscience. And it's telling me that none of this belongs to me, I need to return it."

"Damn conscience. When?"

"January third, around three o'clock. You see, Dr. Fernandez has this theory that my old world has a Slip Sliders Club as well, and it's meeting will be starting about then. So they will help fill me in on the time I missed there, what the other Lola did, for better or worse. He's also made arrangements to be at the Neuse Collider when I slip back. That's where it happens. He will help reorient the other Lola, the one you knew."

"That's not long from now."

Nope."

"Well, I can't believe I'm saying this, but I hope it works."

"Thanks. I'm thinking things will be just as good between you two, maybe better."

"I hope you do well on the other side. Bad choice of words. In your old world."

"Thanks again. You know, I'm looking forward to that first peanut butter and jelly sandwich in a while," said Lola with a grin.

⚠ 🚹 🔗

The two spent New Year's Eve together, bundled up against the cold, in a sea of people waiting for the fireworks display to begin.

"I hope you can help convince the original Lola to keep up the renewed relationship with the Taylors. Jadon really could use a mother now, especially since Caitlin left."

"I'll give it my best."

"It's been quite an adventure, crammed into such a short time, hasn't it."

"Indeed it has," replied Rita as the first rocket rose into the air with an angry hiss.

TWENTY-THREE

🔲 ⚛ ⇄

relidS pilS

Lola and Rita spent the next day, the first day of 2020, reminiscing and watching parades on television. To be fair, Lola's reminiscence didn't extend back very far. Most of it past two months ago was Rita telling Lola what had happened. Lola thought they sounded like some quite happy times. Apart from the quid-pro-quo dalliances, of course.

That Thursday, the second day of 2020, after Rita got home from work, they said their tearful farewells inside apartment 206.

"I'll be at work tomorrow when you—leave."

"It's not like you're totally losing Lola."

No, but I am losing Lola number two."

"Like I said, it'll be fine. Maybe better."

"Sure. I'll have to get used to you remembering shit. Well, there's no use drawing this out, making it harder. Good luck back in your world." They hugged.

As Rita walked out the door, the last time Lola would see her in this world, she thought," *I hope it'll be fine.* Then, *I wonder; there should be a Rita back in my world. Maybe I'll look her up. Maybe I already met her, and don't remember?*

🔲 ⚛ ⇄

Lola sat down at the computer and began typing out a note. In it she explained everything of substance that had happened since the slide, both good and bad, so hopefully she would have few if any surprises. She added with the details of the brokerage account she had set up, and how to transfer money from it to her bank. Then she finished with:

> *Pascal is holding a great deal of money for you. I don't even know how much. I was afraid that if I knew, it might color my*

*decision on whether or not to slide back. As I told Rita, you
don't have to accept all of it, or even any of it, if it makes you
uncomfortable. Pascal may help with ideas on what to do with
the cash, should you choose to accept it. Not wanting to be
preachy here, but maybe no more gambling, unless you know the
outcome like I did? Well, that's not really gambling though is
it?*

*As per your career, you are currently on short-term disability. I
assume you would have no trouble convincing the FAA doctor
your memory and skills have returned. The info re the doctor is
in your e-mail. Rita, and members of the SSC should be able
to fill in any blank areas from the past couple of months. Then
you'll hopefully be flying again.*

*All your passwords are the same now as when you slid, except
for your online banking. I had to reset it to: !am@Sl1pSl1der.*

*It is my sincere hope that you continue to repair the rift between
you and D'Shaun. Jadon really loves and misses you. I guess
you know Caitlin left. She rarely visits.*

*Well, I think that about covers it all, or what I can recall.
Best of luck;*

Alternate You

👤 ⚛ ⇆

The next day, Lola got up out of bed late, and doubts soon
began to clutter her mind. *Is this fair to the other Lola? She doesn't
get a choice to stay or go. Stop it. She will be in a much better situation
than she left.*

She got dressed, had a bowl of cereal, and printed out the
note she wrote for her counterpart. She signed her—their—
actual name under the *Alternate You*. Then she folded it enough
so it would fit in her pants pocket.

I'll stop for lunch on the way, she thought. Lola checked that the apartment was the way she wanted the other Lola to find it, sighed, went out the door for the last time and locked it.

Downstairs, she paused to look at the door to 106 for the last time, with a tinge of sadness. Then she was on her way to the Neuse Collider, depot to her old world.

🚆 ⚛ ⇆

Dr. Fernandez met Lola at the entrance to the Collider. After exchanging greetings, he briefed her on what to do, and what to expect once they were underground in the control room.

"Oh, the actual collider is underground. I thought I was in the wrong place until I saw you. Thanks for coming all the way from Jacksonville."

"You're welcome. Yes, the collider is isolated underground. Now, you're absolutely sure you want to do this?"

"I am. Let's go."

With that they went into the lobby. He got their visitor badges at the security desk, explaining that Lola was the company representative of INPRO, who made the suit they were testing. On the way down in the elevator, he explained to Lola, "I thought about trying to imprint you with the knowledge of how this reversal works, the suit details and all, but given the short timeframe, we really didn't have time for the needed hypnotist sessions. And we haven't yet perfected the Vulcan mind meld."

"Oh, *Star Trek* is a thing here too?"

"*Star Trek*?" After a brief pause, he continued, "yes, it is. Just trying to lighten the moment with a little humor. *Very* little humor."

"About that hypnotist you sent *me* to. It appears he has an ongoing criminal enterprise on the side. In an incredible coincidence, he appears to have partnered up with someone from my alternate past. Someone who turned out to be a pretty shady character. There was an incident where he came after my friend Rita and me, at gunpoint. He was thinking he could pry more about the future out of me," said Lola. "As if he could force me to remember more."

"Oh, sorry. We'll certainly steer clear of Mr. Meinkes," he said as the elevator stopped, the door slowly slid open, and they stepped out into the control room. He was surprised to see more than the professor and Dr. Feirstein. There seemed to be a heated debate going on between Professor Gibbons and one of the strangers.

"I was supposed to be running tests on the suit today."

"I'm sorry, but Dr. Theo had to move up his experiments to this afternoon. He's on the Collider's board of directors, so what he wants, he gets. Who are those two?"

Looking in the direction the man pointed, the professor said, "oh, that's Doctor Fernandez, and the INPRO company rep, Lola Sandborne. They made the suit prototype."

Dr. Fernandez motioned for Professor Gibbons to come over to where he stood, and whispered, "I'm afraid it's time to switch to Plan B. I'll do the talking."

The professor nodded and walked back over to the stranger.

"Doctor..." started Dr. Fernandez

"I'm not a doctor. I'm not a scientist, I'm Richard Brewster, the operations manager here," interrupted the former stranger.

"Mr. Brewster, we really need to perform this test today. You see, Lola here has come a long way from the INPRO headquarters and must get back there this evening. She has to present the test results tomorrow."

"I'm sorry, but it'll have to wait until Doctor Theo is done."

Dr. Fernandez glanced at his watch. It was approaching twenty after three. "And how long will that be?" he asked.

"At least two hours. Say, where's your test mannequin?"

Glances were exchanged between doctor and professor. "Today is—was—to be a live test," interjected the professor. *May as well give up the truth, at least part of it, if there's a chance we can still fit it in.*

"What? No, no, no. I can't condone that. Too dangerous."

"Live tests have to start sometime. We're fairly certain of safety. We just need to test for mobility," replied Professor Gibbons.

"Sorry, but no. But you can stay and observe Dr. Theo's experiments."

Again, Dr. Fernandez conferred quietly with Professor Gibbons. "Plan C," said the doctor.

"And that is?"

After the doctor explained his impromptu plan to the professor, in whispered tones, he asked, "you on board with that?"

Professor Gibbons took a deep breath, exhaled, and said, "Yeah."

"O.K. Take Dr. Feirstein into our confidence."

"Sure."

The professor sidled up to Dr. Feirstein and said, "if you've got a free moment, come with me?"

"Sure."

The professor led him to the control room wall farthest from the collider hatch and control console. Dr. Theo and Richard the manager had their backs to the pair, intently staring at a console screen. The collider was operating.

After the professor clued the doctor in on Plan C, his eyebrows rose, then he nodded in agreement. "O.K. Let's do it," said the physicist. He crossed the room and rejoined the others.

Lola and Dr. Fernandez still stood near the elevator door.

"It's running?" asked Lola.

"Yes."

"I'm surprised it's so quiet."

"Not a lot of moving parts. It's about to get loud in *here* though. When it does, move away from the door and join Professor Gibbons, where he's standing."

"O.K." said Lola, drawing out the letters, sounding perplexed.

Dr. Fernandez, assured that those at the console were intensely occupied, nodded to the professor. He reached out to the wall behind him and his arm moved down. The room suddenly erupted in flashing red light and the sound of a klaxon horn. "Fire. Exit the building quickly but calmly," spoke an automated voice. It added, "Take the stairway exit. The elevators are locked." It then began to repeat the message over and over.

Richard motioned for Dr. Theo to get out of his seat at the console and follow him. He trotted over to the stairway door, beside the elevator. "Everyone out. Now!" he yelled.

Dr. Theo was reluctant to leave. "Shouldn't we shut the collider down?"

"It's shutting itself off, triggered by the fire alarm. Let's go."

"We'll get out via the rear stairs," said Dr. Fernandez, as he headed to a door opposite the one with the elevator and main stairwell. "Doctor, professor, Lola; follow me."

The four entered the rear stairwell, then Dr. Fernandez said, "Let's wait here a few seconds until we're sure they've cleared. Then we go back in. Ready, Lola?"

"Yes, but won't the collider stay off as long as the fire alarm is active?"

"True, but I know a way to override that," said Dr. Feirstein.

Shortly Dr. Feirstein opened the door back up and strode over to the console. "We need to act fast before the fire department comes down here."

Dr. Fernandez stopped to pick up the bag containing the suit, that had been lying on the floor, near the door they just re-entered from. "Let's get you in this," he said to Lola.

The professor stood by the console in front of a closed circuit video monitor.

Dr. Fernandez yelled at Lola, to be heard inside the now fitted suit. "You remember how to open the hatch? And what to do once inside?" She gave a thumbs up.

"Alright then. This is goodbye, and good luck back in your world." He gave her a pat on the shoulder.

With that, Lola strode toward the door, her heart pounding in her chest. She opened the hatch, and stepped through to the alien looking maze of wires and plumbing that made up the large tunnel of the collider. She closed the hatch behind her, and turned left to wait for the signal. *I can do this. I can do this.*

"We're back up," shouted Dr. Feirstein.

"Wow, that was quick. Thanks," Dr. Fernandez said.

Lola saw the red LED flash in her visor. *Point of no return.* With a shaky hand, she turned the valve to release the noble gases into the tunnel, and was nearly blinded.

Just then the video monitor burst with brightness, in a northern lights like display.

"She's showing erratic movement," the professor suddenly shouted. "Shut it down. Now."

After only a few seconds, Dr. Feirstein said, "it's safe now."

The professor ran to the hatch, opened it up, slid inside and chased after a now running Lola. He sped up to get ahead of her, so she could see him. He yelled, "stop! It's O.K." Then, "follow me out of here, and we'll get you out of that suit."

"I'm practically blinded," came the barely perceptible reply from inside the suit.

"Take my hand. I'll guide you."

Back inside the control room, and now out of the suit, Dr. Fernandez once again quipped, "did we get you out of a meeting?"

"As a matter of fact. So, where am I, and how did I get here? And, is this place on fire?"

"You're inside the Neuse Collider, near Raleigh. Back in your original world. How? I'll explain later, and there's no fire. We do need to get up and out of here though. Follow us to the stairway door." Dr. Fernandez took the suit and stuffed it back inside the bag. He offered a hand to Lola, who took it.

"I'll join you shortly. Need to erase the video evidence," said Dr. Feirstein.

When the rest emerged up and out through the rear fire exit, into the waning daylight, they could see red lights flashing around the corner of the building. "I hope the doctor finishes quickly, or he'll have some *splainin* to do," said the professor.

"I assume our counterpart club found you and explained what had happened?"

"Yes. I was quite surprised there were others. And they were a great help."

"We had a member who had slid to a more advanced world, where they had learned to reverse the process. From him, we have been able to replicate it. You're just the second one to come back."

Just then, Dr. Feirstein emerged, saying, "yeah. We just did that," and laughed nervously.

"Oh. Lola. Check your pockets. I believe your counterpart left you a message," said Dr. Fernandez.

She fished out and unfolded the sheet of paper.

When Lola finished with the note, she turned to Dr. Fernandez. "Wow, I'm stunned at what my twin did in such a short time. I didn't really do anything for her, I'm afraid."

"Ah, but that's where you're wrong. I think slipping into your life gave her a sense of purpose and fulfillment that she hadn't had for a long time. I think wherever she is, she is going to enjoy trying to recapture that feeling."

"Oh, I can only hope so." Checking her pockets once again, she came up with a car key. "I hope a jacket's in the car, it's getting quite chilly."

"It's in the front parking lot." the doctor said. Just head toward the flashing fire truck lights."

"Well, I guess it's time to get back to Charlotte. And see what she's done to the place."

"O.K. We'll correspond later. Welcome to the club, Lola. Once again."

Author's Notes

This is mostly a work of fiction. There is some science, and some actual events, weaved into the fiction, however…

Physicists claim that "spooky action at a distance is an actual phenomenon. It simultaneously synchronizes the orientation of paired sub-atomic particles across huge distances. The swapping of minds across great distances was fabricated, of course, including the computer's memory swap.

My condolences to those who were Carolina Panthers fans in 2019. After a decent start at five and three, the team never won another game that year.

There was a major economic collapse in Argentina in 2001. However, the case of a slip slider, Ronaldo DeCantos, knowing beforehand that it would occur is complete fantasy.

The "wisdom of crowds" has been demonstrated by surveys, though the example of guessing the cow's weight was my invention. The "momentum of crowds" belongs under: fiction.

The anecdote about the physicist who was struck by a proton beam in a particle accelerator was true. It happened in the former Soviet Union on July 13, 1978, to particle physicist Anatoli Bugorski. Safety was apparently last in 1970s Soviet Russia. He did indeed survive, in fact, outliving the USSR and going on to earn his PHD.

And, of course, COVID-19 was (is) real. At the time of writing, although I ruled out a laboratory leak in the book, authorities are still unsure of its origin. There is indeed a Wuhan Institute of Virology. The other theory is: infected bat meat from a Wuhan "wet" market.